"Truth must be proven!"

*"Yes, but sometimes truth is in the mind
before evidence can be found.
This is how science proceeds."*

Greg Iles — Footprints of God

THE RODIN QUEST

NEVILLE HALE

To:

[signature] Dec 8th 2006.

Published by

**MELROSE
BOOKS**

An Imprint of Melrose Press Limited
St Thomas Place, Ely
Cambridgeshire
CB7 4GG, UK
www.melrosebooks.com

FIRST EDITION

Cover designed by Sophie Fitzjohn

ISBN 1 905226 64 0

Printed and bound in Great Britain by:
CPI Bath, Lower Bristol Road,
Bath, BA2 3BL, UK

Dedication

This book is dedicated to the loving memory of my wife Marguerite and my sister Molly.

I wish also to dedicate this book to Marguerite's children.

Less than three years after their father's tragic death in a plane crash in 1957, George, Jim and Susan accepted me as their 'dad'. They have given me their unconditional love and support to me for all my years since that time.

Preface

My novel is a romance, or perhaps more accurately two romances, one in England and one in France. They were destined to converge, leading two men to meet in London in 1884-5. One was a resident in London, Theodore Villeneuve, a jeweller and goldsmith. The second, who would much later be world famous, was the French sculptor Auguste Rodin.

The mystery began when it became known to the Villeneuve family that the little black statue standing in the corner of Theodore's living room for so long had, in fact, been accepted by him *in payment of a debt*. More than 100 years were to pass before any Villeneuve descendent showed more than fond but casual interest in her. It was, in fact, an exhibition of Rodin works in Toronto 2001 that sent the *what if* signal to the impossibly naïve author, the most senior Villeneuve descendent; to start digging.

The novel therefore revolves around four years of research in the quest for origin of this beautiful but enigmatic little figure. Inevitably, it seemed only courteous to report this work to The Musee Rodin in Paris from time to time. Whereas we found the Museum to be very cooperative and responsive to general enquiries there was clearly some policy that forbade them from responding *at all* to any possibility that I might actually possess a Rodin, or even a Rodin studio reject.

To keep my novel going I needed to take the liberty of addressing this silence by presenting a *fly-on-the-wall* presence at *fictional* committee meetings addressing controversial policy issues.[1]

I have made every effort to fictionalize *fair and balanced internal debate*. There is no intention to embarrass the Musee Rodin in any way, nor is it to reveal the identity of individuals therein, by position or name.

NH, Thursday, March 16, 2006

Footnotes

1 (The subject has been confined to Chapter 14)

Acknowledgements

My thanks to my 'research team' for their enthusiastic response and support — Patricia Burt, Don and Marg Wightman, Bill and Marsha Barrow, Eileen Butler, Louise Blackhurst, Bruce Anderson and Robert Fortin.

In particular there are a few special members who made specific advancements in my Quest to prove Rodin's involvement in my Black Statue. **Dale Dunning**, sculptor who found the internet link that tied the puzzling bronze sheath to experiments by Rodin in the 1881-4 period that led to the electroplating technique used in the bronzing of the Black Statue. **Terry Gamble**, (my 'devil's advocate personified' throughout) who insisted on me finding a way to obtain X-rays. For the X-rays themselves I owe special thanks to **Jim Bell DVM**, our local veterinarian. (Amazing and unexpected results). **Nancy Green** for linking me to the Canadian Conservation Institute (CCI) and subsequently to **Jane Sirois**, senior conservation scientist, who's work revealed unusual and important characteristics from samples of moulding material taken from the Black Statue.

On the need for provenance, **Donald Combe**, author and expert ancestry researcher 'found' my great grandfather Theodore Villeneuve, which led to my good fortune of contact with **Sheila Jones** at www.ukonline.co.uk and to the revelation of the whole Villeneuve line and other important provenance issues.

Frederic Grunfeld for writing the definitive biography — *RODIN: A Biography*, which became my primary source of information on the Rodin side of the equation for my story.

Sarah Milroy — art critic – Globe and Mail — for her provocative article and critique of the 2001 Rodin Exhibit in Toronto, *From Plaster to Bronze*, that generate my first "What if?"

Austin Kehoe — commissioning editor, and all the staff at Melrose Books, UK — for creating such an enjoyable path towards the publishing of this book.

Contents

Contents

I
Raisin d'être

The purpose of this book is to attempt to solve all the riddles leading to a meeting between Rodin and Villeneuve in London about 1884 and the significance of the statue Villeneuve received.

My statue, known by the family simply as the 'Black Statue', came into family ownership in the 1880's when my great grandfather, Theodore Villeneuve, a London jeweler and goldsmith, accepted the statue "as payment of a debt".

Over the years, visitors to my home occasionally

asked about my statue. I came to replying with a casual "that's my lost Rodin". It was good for an occasional polite chuckle. I chose Rodin because he was the only nineteenth century sculptor I really could recall. He was the only one who was high-profile enough to have a child take notice, as I apparently did in the 1920's and 30's.

It was only when the Rodin exhibition came to Toronto's Royal Ontario Museum in the fall of 2001, along with the publicity that surrounded it, that I got the first inkling … what if?

If we should have reason to believe that the Black Statue is linked to the Rodin studio, the question is: why would a French sculptor run up a debt in London, to be settled by a piece of his work that he had to haul all the way from Paris?

There are a few speculative possibilities to this. Maybe it wasn't a debt, but more likely, barter for jewelry. Maybe it wasn't the artist at all but another person who had acquired the statue from … anywhere! Who's to say it was 'a Rodin', anyway? A rational person might shrug this off as unsolvable. But I was retired and had time on my hands.

The Black Statue was a member of my family household back to the very earliest of my memories. She always stood on a pedestal in a safe corner of our sitting room in London. The furniture was arranged so that I couldn't knock the statue flying as I rode my tricycle around the house. This had been her spot ever since my parents married in January 1919 and my grandmother, Isabella Villeneuve Hale, passed the Black Statue on as a wedding present.

When the London Blitz started in 1940, my father, an architect, and I, a budding engineer at 18, held a conference on where to put the Black Statue for safety. The unanimous conclusion was the cupboard under the stairs. We reasoned that the staircase was the strongest structure and *should* hold up when the rest of the house collapsed. She was wrapped in a blanket and laid on the floor immediately under the second step from the bottom.

When the raid moved overhead, the four of us in the family packed ourselves into the same cupboard. We were packed like sardines and had to sit leaning forward at the staircase angle. I remember my sister piping up: "Hey daddy! It's a good job we don't have a *spiral* staircase!" We all had a good laugh.

For most of the winter of '40–41, there were raids most nights. At the weekends, my dad and I would go for a walk to spot where the bombs had fallen the previous night. When we got home I plotted the sites on a town map. Time and again one could join the dots and draw a curve through them. This defined the flight path of the bomber as it started its turn for home and let its stick of bombs go. One could then project where the next bomb would have been if there had been one more in the stick. It was a bit sobering when, after one raid, this indicated our road (theoretically) as 'ground zero'. "There, but for the grace of God go we."

It was strange how one could be coldly analytical yet not believe *it* would really happen. On our walks we would see, time and again, collapsed homes and through the rubble there stood the staircase. When I look back it seems so callous that we could feel so gratified that our analysis was proven right. *It seemed there was no time to ponder the poignant staircases leading to nowhere; nor the fate of the owner and his family!*

The Black Statue and the family all survived the London Blitz in 1940 as well as the VI's and V2's in 1944–5, despite a number of near-misses. In 1948, at age 26, I emigrated to Canada. She [the statue] remained in England until my father died in 1954. When my mother came to Canada to live with me in 1955 she had a 'steamer-trunk' of possessions. Buried among the clothes, there was the Black Statue, safe and sound. I became the custodian. She stands now in the corner of my living room in Collingwood, Ontario, a safe spot, on the shores of the great lakes at Georgian Bay. The furniture is arranged to cordon the statue off from myself or my friends from staggering or gesticulating with a stick or a crutch.

For the first time I confided in a few friends that I was going to do a bit of serious research on Rodin.

The thought of a 'lost Rodin' seemed to spark interest among friends. It was a great conversation starter. As time went on, and I had a bit more knowledge to banter around, many elected to help with suggestions as well as with their time.

By 2004 we had become a growing research team. So from now on I will talk of "we", not "I". (see Acknowledgments.)

An early benefit from the team effort resulted in a meeting with Dale Dunning – practicing sculptor of repute. He had his own foundry and created his own bronze works by the lost-wax process – essentially the same process used by Rodin.

At our meeting, I recalled to Dale, that when I was still a child, my father told me that the Black Statue was "bronze over plaster". By weight alone, one could tell that it wasn't a cast bronze. It was this outer coating that left Dale and myself wondering how the bronze was applied. What technology sources were in existence that long ago? We couldn't resolve this on the spot.

I got an email from Dale the next day, on August 11, 2004. The message was exciting indeed. While lying in bed that night he concluded that the *only possible explanation* to the bronze coating was electroplating. But could it possibly have been electroplated that many years ago?

Next morning he searched it on the internet. "Low and behold not only was it possible but that it was a popular 19th century technique also known as galvano-plastique". The website that he passed on to me, went on to state that Rodin had used the technique experimentally on one of his plasters of St. Jean Baptiste.[1] After so much wishful thinking on my part, this news was a first sign that there *just might be a possible link* between the Black Statue and the Rodin studio.

This tenuous link between the Black Statue and the fact that Rodin was known to have experimented with metallization of plaster casts, urged me to investigate the life and times surrounding Rodin's early days. One needs a realistic 'stage setting' to work from.

In the 1860's and 1870's, France was undergoing a period of great poverty. Rodin, like nearly all artists in Paris, had virtually no money; he was still an unknown and his works commanded little value.

In 1870, the Franco-Prussian war broke out and soon Paris was under siege, one that lasted 132 days. All able-bodied males were conscripted into the National Guard, constantly alert for an attack that never came. Starvation was rampant. "Food and fuel became scarce and misery and cold became almost unendurable."

In January, 1871, the exhausted city capitulated to the Germans and the first food shipments reached the starving population. Rodin was invalided out of the service on account of myopia: *"The eyes with which he was to create the best known images of France during the next forty years of peace, were considered too feeble to serve the nation in time of war".*[2]

In 1871, Rodin, leaving his partner Rose and child in Paris, moved north to Brussels where he obtained employment as an ornamentalist by day while pursuing his own work by night. He remained there for six years before returning to Paris.

Towards the end of this period, Rodin created his first great work that was to become the talk of the art world. *'L'Age d'arien'* or *'Age of Bronze'*, was a male nude. The model was a Flemish soldier named Auguste Nyet (borrowed from the ranks on special leave). The work was so lifelike that Rodin was accused of *making moulds from life*. This ignited a scandal that was totally unfounded but nevertheless promoted by the art establishment in Paris to hold back this controversial and outstanding artist. A threat to the status quo, Rodin was deeply hurt by the malicious publicity. However, the publicity helped catapult him into public awareness and the beginnings of fame. His next major work was St. Jean Baptiste, created in plaster in 1879. A cast bronze version followed in 1880. In the early 1880's he started experimenting with electroplating that culminated in a 'bronze-over-plaster' version of St. Jean Baptiste.[2]

In a later chapter it will become apparent that very specialized scientific knowledge, equipment and operator-skills are needed for electroplating, especially electroplating of non-conductive materials. *This was not the job for the artist alone.*

Footnotes

1 http:/www.members.authorsguild.net/cnadelman/
2 'RODIN. *A biography*', page 66, Frederic Grunfeld.

2

The Sorcerer

My introduction to Rodin in a serious sense began when the Royal Ontario Museum (ROM) opened an exhibition of Rodin sculptures in Toronto, September 2001.

More specifically, it was an article by Sarah Milroy, art critic to the national newspaper 'The Globe & Mail' that appeared on the weekend of September 22, 2001 when my first "what if?" thought became lodged in my brain. Sarah Milroy, however, warned that "the deeper you dig into Rodin, the further into the hall of mirrors you find yourself".[1] With forty years of prodigious output and hundreds of biographical books and articles on Rodin's extraordinary life and times, it made sense that I should only focus on the facts and innuendo that impacted upon the story I have to tell. It is only fair to add that I approach this subject as an amateur with absolutely no formal qualification as a writer on 'art'.

Rodin had three distinct phases in his life as a sculptor. Life before Camille 1860s–1881; life with Camille 1882–1894; life after Camille 1895–1917. Before and after Camille, Rodin focused on the idolization of the human form, religious and political themes. This was not so during his life with Camille.

During his 12-year turbulent affair with Camille, herself a rising talent in her own right as a sculptor, Rodin's sculpture started to turn from idolization to singular thought. Love changed his life and the characteristics of his work.

As Rodin entered the 1880s, he thought of himself as a humble workman, one fortunate enough to indulge in the work he loved, yet work that would provide enough income to adequately take care of his partner Rose and their young son Auguste. It took others to recognize his genius and to urge him to expand his vision in promoting his own work. This expansion drew him to London on frequent occasions where he gradually, almost against his own will, started to build fame and eventually (after 1900) great wealth.

Rodin's work in the early years was dominated by the brooding figure of 'The Thinker' as the centre piece for the massive 'Gates of Hell' portal. 'Gates', as it was referred to, was never finished. There was this huge portal that surrounded 'The Thinker' with dozens of figure of all shapes and sizes, writhing around in agony.

Brooding and *agony* were joined by works of tragedy, such as the *'Burghers of Calais'* ... five bedraggled men on their way to execution.

This was all heavy stuff, leaving many with the memory that *this and this alone* represented 'Rodin'. This memory spawned comments about my Black Statue. "No, you don't have a Rodin." I even said this myself when I visited the ROM in 2001. The oppressive feeling was overpowering.

When the change took place, the *'Camille effect'* could not be a sudden thing. It was more of a gradual impregnation of *singular thoughts and beauty* into this world of *gloom and tragedy*, as Rodin discovered romantic love and related eroticism. At its peak in about 1885, a 'Rodin' represented *unadorned beauty*.

There were titillating stories regarding Rodin's sculptural techniques. It was said that as he worked his eyes were 'glued' to the model while his hands moulded the figure un-watched. It seemed as if his fingers had *eyes of their own*. His technique was akin to a concert pianist who *glued his eyes* to the music, while his hands (un-watched) transformed his reading into music-to-the-ears.

Rodin's myopia required him to approach the model from time to time, and run his fingers over a particular detail as if to 'program' his fingers. He would then return to the work-in-progress and transfer this tactile information into the sculpture. It was said that this, on occasion, drove the model into passion, sometimes Rodin also.

It was not surprising that in the *Camille* period, many erotic works were produced. The famous 'Kiss' was one of these.

Rodin with 'The Kiss'

One reason why the work of Rodin becomes a *hall of mirrors* was brought about by his passion for replication. In the case of 'The Kiss', first shown in marble in 1887, it is on record that between 1898 and 1917 there were 319 reproductions authorized by the studio. 'The Kiss' was a 'theme', within which a number of different poses and versions, were exhibited. More than one model seems to have claim to fame as *the* model for this masterpiece.

RODIN in his studio

Rodin standing in his studio among his plasters, Anonymous photographer, Gelatin silver print, Collection of Musée Rodin, Paris, Ph 203

Rodin, as a man, came across to me as one of kindness and integrity, that is to say integrity relative to the life and times of the whole artistic community of Paris in the 1800's. One could have countless 'meaningless relationships' with models, yet treat ones true-loves with unquestioned lifetime love and support, as was the case for Rodin with Rose and Camille.

To me, Rodin came across as a genial and humble person who gently tried to tactfully resist his promoters who urged him in the direction of fame and fortune. He tried to avoid confrontation whenever possible.

Other Viewpoints: Edmond de Goncourt, critic, commented: *"Rodin strikes me as a man of projects, sketches, scattering himself in a thousand directions in his fantasies and dreams.*[2, 3]

Footnotes

1 Sarah Milroy article *'RODIN truly a bust'*, September 22, 2001, *Globe & Mail*.
2 *'RODIN. A Biography'*, Frederic Grunfeld, Henry Holt and Company, New York.
3 Pictures from brochure *'Rodin - Magnificent obsession'*, Calgary 2004.

3

The Sorcerer's Apprentice

Courtesy – Musée Rodin – Paris
Photo – César – 1883.

In 1882, Camille Claudel arrived in Paris, leaving the family home in the village of Villeneuve-sur-Fère, half way between Paris and Reims. At age 17 she was confident of her skills in sculpture, she was confident in her beauty and intent on making a name for herself in the artistic hub of Paris.

Her father, Louis-Prosper Claudel, had a respectable position as the registrar of mortgages.

Her mother, *née* Louise Antenaise Cerveaux, was the daughter of a doctor from Picardie. They were solid middle class. Their daughter Camille, at a very early age, became obsessed by everything to do with sculpture. The whole household revolved around her improvised atelier (studio workshop). Her brother Paul, four years younger, felt that she exercised a *cruel influence* on his childhood. Everyone was expected to do her bidding. She learned how to carve marble and then taught one of the housemaids, Eugénie, how to rough out marble blocks like any *metteur au point*.[1]

At the age of thirteen she came to the notice of Alfred Boucher, an artist who had made a name for himself while still in his twenties, who coached her until she left for Paris in 1882.

Once in Paris, her parents realized that they could not afford to support her. Undeterred, Camille organized a colony of young students to share the cost of studio space and modeling fees. Before leaving for other assignments, Alfred Boucher arranged for his friend Paul Dubois to continue to give her counsel and the advice that had already produced such estimable results.[2]

As a one-time guest lecturer to Camille's colony, Rodin noticed an outstanding talent in Camille. Soon after this brief encounter, Camille knocked on Rodin's door applying as an assistant in the Rodin studio. Rodin took her in firstly as a pupil, soon to be promoted to assistant.

It so happened that in 1881, Rodin received a commission to produce 'The Gates of Hell', a mammoth undertaking for a huge portal that was to include dozens of individual sculptures that became attached to the structure. 'The Thinker' became the centerpiece. This was a project that needed a dedicated studio of its own, based on size alone. It was a project that was never finished. This might have been partly due to Rodin repeatedly deciding to remove figures, from time to time, for individual sale, or as he put it, "to give them a life of their own".

After Camille had been with the studio for more than a year Rodin asked, one day, if she would consider modeling for figures he needed for 'Gates'.

Camille heard the request, but continued silently with her detail work for a few moments. "Monsieur, I am a sculptor, not a model." Rodin replied: "That is the very reason why I make the request. Paris is full of beautiful young models. I have worked with many of them. They carry out my instructions but their eyes remain vacant. They neither know nor care what emotion I am trying to portray. I have given you, Mademoiselle, the responsibility to detail hands and feet for my statues because you know how to express the meaning of my theme through your intuitive understanding and skill as a sculptor. My thought was that together the model and the sculptor become the matching of the minds to a common cause. Ideas can be generated and refined by this combination and interplay between the two minds". Again a few minutes of silence as Camille pondered. Then she spoke:

"How do you know that my body will meet your requirements, Monsieur? I have never posed before, either dressed or nude." There was something in the way that she seemed so matter-of-fact for an eighteen-year-old, so un-shy, that intrigued Rodin. She spoke with confidence. She knew the power of her own sensuality and beauty. Rodin replied: "I know how you move, Mademoiselle, I see your instinctively proud carriage. To move in that way you need a perfect physique, the balance must be perfect". Camille drew a deep breath then exhaled slowly:

"Monsieur Rodin, I understand and respect your reasons for making this request. I therefore have one condition for you to consider. I *may be* agreeable to posing on a case-by-case basis; but I too would need to be equally convinced that the subject you wish to portray is also the subject that I wish to portray. I can assure you; you will not find me posing with 'vacant eyes'. With a little smile, Camille asked Rodin: "While you are considering this Monsieur, I ask you to turn your back for a moment or two". Models do not make that request, and would be rebuffed if they did. But Camille was a sculptor prepared to go beyond the call of duty, albeit on a case-by-case basis! She removed her clothes and walked to one end of the studio. "You may turn around Monsieur," she said as she started pirouetting slowly towards him with graceful arm movements, sometimes outstretched horizontally, sometimes right-arm raised, displaying her ballet training as a child. Rodin immediately recognized that Camille was just as unabashed in displaying her sensuality personally as she had been when working in clay. With a final pirouette she came to rest before him in a modest pose ... though her eyes remained open and were not vacant!

Thus a stormy ten-year professional and personal relationship slowly began to develop. This was the beginning of a unique collaboration between two great artists, one the sculptor, the other the model/ sculptress; two minds locked onto a singular thought. This was the relationship that created the finest of erotic masterpieces of all time; 'The Kiss' (1886), 'Faun and Nymph' (The Monotour) (1886), 'Metamorphoses of Ovid' (1886), 'The Eternal Idol' (1889) and finally 'Despair' (1890). The following brief excerpt from the Fredric Grunfeld 'RODIN' biography provides an insightful glimpse of that time:

"It was an immensely exciting time for both of them. On Rodin's side, the ebb and flow of their affair could almost be charted by the rise and fall of the number of erotic images which he produced between 1882 and 1894. Some had titles and the entire spectrum of sensualism from 'Le Baiser' to 'La Fatigue' ... but countless others were part of a great outpouring of anonymous clay sketches which he was perpetually modifying, transforming, destroying and which he referred to as his "embryos".[3]

As the love affair progressed, Rodin's style fell more and more under Camille's magic spell.

"We know Camille's hand whenever we see instantaneous design (as opposed to Rodin's long-agonized arrangement) or where we see demure sweet innocence (as opposed to melodrama lacking in emotional candor). We know Camille's input when we see a pose that makes sense to a dancer's eyes (Rodin's earlier and later works do not make sense). It is obvious to anyone who studied movement instead of pose".[4]

Courtesy – Musée Rodin – Paris

The period in which Rodin and Camille were together became known as Rodin's 'sweet' period. But it was not sweet all the time. Rodin was inclined to imply that all ideas were his alone and no credit was given to Camille. She worked hard to develop her own unique style, one that broke with tradition and formed a modern new trend. As time went on, she realized that she needed to escape the shadow of the "mighty Rodin". Two, among many, outstanding works evolved, 'The Flute-Player' and 'The Waltz'. Some critics suggest that Camille's flowing 'Waltz' was the "perfect bridge" from the classical to art nouveau.[4]

Courtesy – Musée Rodin
– Paris
Sculptures by Camille Claudel

Postscript

Whereas Camille's influence on Rodin was unquestioned, the erotic nature of their work during this period caused Camille to be identified with the erotic also. This may have finally been her undoing. When she eventually branched out on her own in the early 1890s she found that it was one thing for Parisian society to accept eroticism from male sculptors, *but from a sculptress?*

Footnotes

1 'RODIN. A Biography'. Frederic Grunfeld, 1987, pages 211–212.
2 'RODIN. A Biography', Frederic Grunfeld, 1987 pages 212–213.
3 'RODIN. A Biography', Frederic Grunfeld, 1987, page 221.
4 http.//www.cs.wustl.edu/~loui/Camille

4

The Specialist

PARIS – February 24, 1881

New Yorker J. Danielli stepped off the Boat-Train on his arrival in Paris from London. It was late afternoon.

A few days earlier he had arrived at Southampton, England by steamship directly from New York. He had journeyed by train to London with a personal mission to visit the British Museum and the famous, albeit controversial, Elgin Marbles. These were the ancient Greek Statue-collection that the British so imperiously decided to take out of Greek hands to protect them from the harsh Greek environment, or perhaps more specifically, from the Greeks themselves, since the London environment isn't any better than the Greek. But the British felt they knew what was best for Greek statues (to name just one item).

As soon as his curiosity and appreciation had been satisfied, Danielli was impatient to be on his way to Paris to get on with his main purpose for undertaking all this travel. He found a small quiet little hotel on Rue de Berre, just off the Champs-Elysees. If his trip proved successful, he would need to find a permanent lodging since the work to be undertaken would keep him in Paris for a considerable period of time.

Danielli, the youngest son of Italian immigrant parents, though only 25 years old, had a confident air of a man, well-educated and successful in his many endeavors. Primarily, he was an entrepreneur with a chemical and electrical engineering background. He had a good ear for languages and spoke fluently in French, albeit with a New York accent. He had spent the last four years on the Thomas Edison research team in New York, working on electrical power distribution development, the newest of the new technologies in this rapidly changing world. The work was demanding. Their competitors were the George Westinghouse group, also in the U.S.A., and the Werner Von Siemens group in Germany. Once contracts were being let, the pressure subsided to some extent for the technical staff.

Danielli's work experience had inspired an idea that laid dormant in his mind for some time. He now wished to promote it. He would need the cooperation of a high profile sculptor, to first prove and then launch his invention. His target was obvious. He needed Auguste Rodin as a partner. Rodin was undoubtedly the finest of the new wave of French sculptors. His reputation held up well among the many contemporary 'Future Greats, in the arts ... Degas, Van Gogh, Gauguin, Monnet ... the list goes on.

PARIS – February 25, 1881

Danielli walked to Rodin's studio from the hotel about mid afternoon. The day was cool but sunny. The door was answered by a lady to whom Danielli presented his calling card. "Madame, would you be good enough to ask Monsieur Rodin if he could spare me a few minutes of his time. Tell him, if you will, that I wish to talk about a new technology that might interest him." She nodded and asked him to wait while she presented the card and delivered the message.

Moments later, Rodin himself walked briskly towards Danielli. He was wearing an overall stained with plaster and a floppy black beret on his head, equally soiled. Smiling, he wiped his hands on his sides then offered one to Danielli. They shook hands affably and energetically.

"Monsieur Danielli, you must excuse my appearance, sculpture is a messy game and I have to keep moving, to use the materials I have prepared whilst they remain fresh. But please come in. Though my eyes and hands will have to keep busy, I can assure you, Monsieur, that my ears will be dedicated to hearing what you have to say. New York to Paris is a long way to travel, you must have something good to tell me, no?" They laughed. Danielli immediately felt at ease.

Danielli spoke: "Monsieur, to get straight to the point, you are no doubt aware that earlier in this century it became possible to coat base metals with precious

Rodin
courtesy Musée Rodin

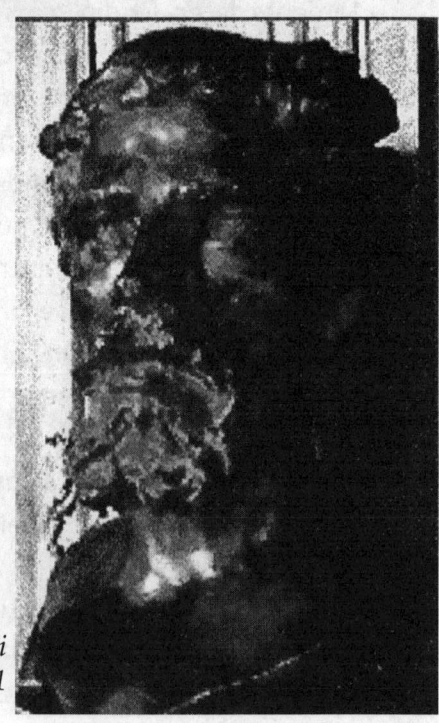

J. Danielli
J. Danielli By Rodin 1881

metals such as gold on brass, silver over copper and so forth, using a galvanic process known as electroplating. Due to lack of sufficiently reliable electrical power at the time, the process was limited to small jewelry items. In the last four years, I have had the privilege of working under Thomas Edison in the United States, on the development of power distribution to cities, industries and eventually private homes. This opened up a whole host of possibilities". Rodin looked up from his work and nodded, ready to hear more.

"I realized that now electroplating was no longer limited to small jewelry items. With sufficient electrical power, plating would be possible for 'man-size' objects." After a moment or two Danielle continued: "There was one further possibility that seemed to have been overlooked. What if one could electroplate, or metallize materials other than base metals? Suppose, Monsieur, one could perhaps produce a gold statue at less cost than that of a cast bronze statue produced by present techniques?"

This was the time to pause. Danielli knew he had Rodin's full attention, not just his ears but his whole being! Rodin had downed tools and now ushered Danielli to a corner of the studio where a pair of plaster-stained arm chairs awaited. A bottle of Bordeaux and two glasses stood on a table that separated the chairs. With a silent enquiry and a silent raise of the eyebrows and smile from Danielli, Rodin poured the wine.

Rodin settled back and smiled. "You tell a very good story Monsieur Danielli. I am sure that you haven't come all this way without persuasive evidence to overcome

27

my incredulity as to what I have just heard." It was Danielli's turn to smile as he reached in his pocket and pulled out a golden egg and rolled it across the table surface into Rodin's reach.

Rodin picked up the egg. "Well, it certainly looks like gold and feels like gold, but it weighs practically nothing". Danielli replied: "It is a plaster casting that has been gold-plated. It is 23 carat gold but its thickness is less than one-tenth of a millimetre. When one considers that the typical shell thickness of a casting by the lost-wax process is about 5 mm, the saving in the amount of metal needed for a statue of the same size and identical appearance is about 50 to 1".

Rodin wagged his head, took a deep breath and slowly exhaled. "I had always understood that one couldn't plate plaster." Danielli replied: "That was always true until I invented what I inspiringly have named the 'Danielli Method'. Monsieur, you have the first sample in your hand".

After a few moments, Danielli stood. "Monsieur Rodin, you have graciously allowed me to interrupt your work. I suggest that I leave now while your materials are, I hope, still workable. Suppose we have another meeting within a few days. Then we might discuss an exclusivity arrangement such that we can explore the technology together at our leisure while guarding our mutual advantage over others." Rodin, needing to get back to work, picked up his glass. "A toast, Monsieur Danielli ... until we meet again."

As Danielli strolled back up the Champs Elysees

towards Rue de Berre, he felt pleased with his strategy of leaving Rodin *ready for more*. In the meantime there were a number of matters to attend to. The most important of these was to get in contact with the French Power Station committee. All the major capitals of the world would be competing to be the first with bright street lighting, the lighting of public buildings and the illuminating of the statues in the squares. That would only be the beginning. The use of the power once it was available would be the big prize.

Having worked for Thomas Edison on the winning contender proposal for lighting up the large cities, he expected his credibility to be recognized by the local authorities. He would be offering his services to the committee as it planned the first stage of this technical revolution. His service might be as a technical consultant. Alternatively, he might consider a place on the committee, providing it included an adequate source of income. Or he might become an employee if such an arrangement would leave him enough time to also pursue his project with Rodin. One way or another he needed a paying job as well as some time of his own. In the meantime, he felt he had done enough for the day and he headed to the hotel bar for a coffee and brandy. He needed a quiet time to rehearse his plans.

Apart from survival money, the reason for trying to get involved with the power distribution group was to negotiate his use of a small area on their premises for him to set up an electroplating laboratory and workshop. The point was, he need access to the power *now*...where better than at the power station? It could be months or years before power was broadly available throughout Paris in homes or in privately-rented industrial buildings.

Danielli recalled in his mind, the discussion he had with his father, the night before heading to Europe. The whole family had much respect for Danielli-senior. He had no imposing credentials but he had a shrewd mind. He immediately demonstrated this, on hearing Danielli's plan.

Danielli-senior thought for a bit and then said: "Son, you have spent four or more years as one of the few privileged men working under the great Thomas Edison to develop a new technology that will clearly change the world for ever-and-a-day. I cannot understand why you would now choose to squander this knowledge and opportunity by concentrating on such a minute technical niche as electroplating plaster. This is especially so since you only appear to have one customer, one man, in mind!"

"Well, father, when you put it that way, this does need some sort of defence and, hopefully, some rationalization on my part. First of all, I am confident that I can go to Paris or, for that matter, any capital of the world and obtain a good position in furthering Edison's work. I am intensely interested in this. My invention, on the other hand, for being able to electroplate plaster or any other non-conductive material, is not a world-shaker. However it is of keen interest to me. The year I spent in Greece before I went with Edison, including the nine months I spent studying Greek sculpture and anatomy at Athens University, made me realize that there is more to life than a high-powered career. For now let us call this my hobby. I believe I can satisfy both objectives for now. I can look beyond having Mr. Rodin as my only customer. I see a big market for art reproductions. The 'Danielli Method' may eventually be the key to quality reproductions of famous works of art at an affordable price to the common man. My journey to Paris is to arrange for Rodin, an outstanding artist, to draw the attention of the public by using and showing confidence in my idea."

Danielli-Senior nodded: "I am satisfied for now, son. You seem to have thought this through, at least in the near-term. There is nothing like having two strings to your bow. I wish you God speed". They clasped hands and then embraced.

As Danielli thought of this conversation he felt a twinge of guilt. His father was fairly old now and did not realize that his youngest son might be away for a matter of years.... not weeks, not months, *years*. Young Danielli felt that it would break both of their hearts to have to part with that knowledge in their minds. "If Rodin had rejected me (and he still could), I would be home the next month. Why risk that?"

The reason for a long absence from home was

that the electroplating was a highly specialized technology. It would be necessary for Danielli to 'baby it along' until the day came when Rodin would appear with one of his famous statues, having exactly the visual qualities of his famous bronzes from the Rudier Foundry, patina and all.

Danielli also knew that Rodin would need to be handled with 'kid-gloves' when he found that Danielli's special plaster, that he named 'malleable marble', would be needed instead of regular plaster. Then there was also the special coating of the plaster surface to make it conductive. Great artists of Rodin's caliber might wish to resist these *new-fangled* things. Danielli further realized that he would have to keep it low-profile so far as Rodin's important clients were concerned. The wealthy collectors would certainly shy away from the lightweight versions of Rodin's work, even if they did look identical. For them, money was usually no object!

Danielli mused that if he were ever invited to make recommendations on how to manage a great artist such as Rodin it might be as follows: the maitre would continue to produce his great works by his classical methods, signed, numbered and appearing in public in small limited editions. These would be sold to governments, museums, wealthy collectors. Their value would be supported by their rarity and traceability. The maitre's studio would also have a separate division staffed with artisans. Their task would be to produce larger limited editions in the same scale and also numbered but not signed. This group would be produced using the 'Danielli Method' of electroplating plaster casts. These would have an authorization studio mark and be available for sale at a price affordable to the middle class. Finally, the electroplating industry might bid for the right to mass-produce small versions of the original work. They might be cheap base-metal castings with the manufacturers stamp. This source would have no direct link to the Maitre's studio. They would supply the 'trinket market' under copyright law.

Danielli must keep his legacy in mind – art in the homes of the middle class.

In due course, Rodin and Danielli developed a partnership that owned the patent rights to the 'Danielli Method'. Quite early on, Rodin suggested that the 'Danielli Method' name should be changed now that he was an equal partner. He offered: "For example, we could combine letters from both our names." He took a piece of card, tore it in half and printed 'DAN' on one half and on the other 'RO'. He put them side by side to spell 'DANRO'; 'the danro method'. When Danielli showed little enthusiasm for this idea, Rodin switched the card round to spell 'RODAN'. "Well, at least Monsieur, you get one unshared letter out of five!" He roared with laughter, slapping Danielli on the back. The cavernous studio rocked with the booming echo. After a few seconds of hesitation, Danielli joined in, at first rather weakly, but gathering volume as he became more confident of Rodin's *puckish* humour. "Now, back to business." It was decided after some friendly argument that the name 'Galvano Plastique' be used. 'Galvano' obviously linked to the 'galvanic action', the basis of electroplating. It also had an Italian connotation that linked to the name Danielli. 'Plastique' had a French as well as a 'plaster' connotation which satisfied Rodin.

Rodin and Danielli became close friends both professionally and socially. A short excerpt about this relationship appears under 'notes' in Frederic Grunfeld's 'RODIN. A biography'.[1,2]

It is believed that experiments were occasional events, probably giving way to more urgent tasks, until 1884 or possibly into 1885. The final cast was undoubtedly the Galvano Plastique version of St. Jean Baptiste. During this period the technology was limited to exclusive use by the Rodin studio. Rodin probably decided at that point not to include Galvano Plastique with his serious work. He and Danielli may then have drifted apart.

Footnotes

1 In 1881–2, Rodin had a commission to produce a bust of J. P. Laurens, a great French artist in his day. He also had a commission to produce a bust of Alphonse Legros, the great etcher and French painter, who lived in London. A third bust, that

Rodin felt motivated to produce, was that of his friend and colleague, Danielli.

2 The Grunfeld biography commented on this as follows: "The Danielli bust was more conventional – a portrait of the young man who had invented a galvanic process for bronze-plating plaster, the 'Danielli Method', which Rodin used experimentally for bronze-plating one of his St. Jean casts. Danielli, who was also an expert in ceramics and Greek sculpture, founded the firm of 'J. Danielli Jeune, 108 Boulevard St. Germain', where he sold 'malleable marble' [3] and undertook the metallization of plaster casts. For several years he and Rodin were on the best of terms: once when he invited Mme. Rodin to lunch just as the sculptor was on his way to London, Rose was told ' I hope my darling that to please me you'll go on Sunday to have lunch with Monsieur Danielli'. It was not often that Rose was sent to deputize for the maitre."

3 There seems to be no trace of a material known as 'malleable marble'. It might have been a precursor of plasticine (which first appeared on the market about 1900) or it might have been a plaster that was malleable in the early stages, then hardening to a marble-like rigidity when cured. It probably didn't sell, and vanished without leaving any impact on history.

5

The Villeneuve Bloodline

As I worked away on this book it gradually dawned on me that I now knew a great deal more about Rodin than I did about my great grandfather. In point of fact, I knew so little that I had to dig out my late-sister's memoirs to find out that great grandfather Villeneuve was christened Theodore.

The Villeneuve bloodline was on my father's side. There were huge differences between my mother's and my father's family. My mother was a Johnson, one of a large closely-knit Victorian family. It seemed that nearly all the Johnson clan were living their lives in Richmond-upon-Thames, 12 miles west of London. In consequence, though spending my first three years in central London ("born within the sound of Bow bells"), I grew up in the midst of the Johnson clan. I had countless cousins, aunts and uncles as well as a good smattering of great aunts and great uncles. My sister and I had a comfortable feeling of love and security in those bygone days.

My father's family was totally different. There was my father, much loved and respected, and his mother, Isabella Henrietta Susannah Hale, nee Villeneuve. There seemed to be no one else.

When Molly and I asked our dad to tell us about grandpa Hale, he would strangely, but kindly, sidestep the issue. All we got to know was that he was a cabinet maker and that he died at age 52 in 1909. With so little in facts, Molly and I invented our own. Even years later when Isabella was resident in our home, and at the time of her death in 1940, her last words were *"I didn't mean it I didn't mean it!"*. We were to later speculate ... was there a hidden secret perhaps concerning Edward Hales' short life?

We got to know a tiny bit about great grandpa Villeneuve. He was jeweler specializing in gold and also in filigree jewelry. We were told he was French and that he married a girl from Prussia shortly after they met in London 'way-back-when'. They lived out their entire married lives, in the Clerkenwell district of Central London. It was said that she 'ruled the roost' and decreed that only German would be spoken in the home. In consequence, Isabella, the eldest daughter, my grandmother, had a strong German accent all her life yet she never set foot outside England. She also 'endeared herself' to the British by frequently declaring proudly that she "didn't have a drop of English blood in her veins".

We well remembered being told that the little Black Statue that stood in the corner of the 'sitting room' was accepted by great-grandpa Villeneuve in settlement of a debt. Oh yes, one more thing: family lore had it that Theodore journeyed on foot across Europe carrying a big stick to fend off robbers. We were never told why he had to do this. If he lived in France he would have to be heading East or North. Where would he be going?

With that sparse background, it was high time we started an ancestry search. I phoned Donald Combe[1] asking for a few pointers on how to get started. I told him I was looking to find an ancestor named Theodore Villeneuve. He was born in France about 1840 and he was a jeweler. Within 24 hours Donald called me to say he had found a Theodore Villeneuve *but it seemed the place was wrong and he was born much earlier.* "This man was born in Germany in 1822!" After a long pause he said, "Oh yes! He was also a jeweler". With all the inaccurate information that I had given Donald, my great grandfather had, in fact, been located. This was incredible!

I remained staggered, not to say devastated, by the news that Theodore may not have been a Frenchman. I was advised to research the Huguenot migration, the result of the harassment of Protestants by the Catholics in France that occurred in the 1500s and 1600s. (The term 'harassment' was rather mild when one read that a Huguenot in the wrong place at the wrong time was customarily burned at the stake.) So there was an impetus to move East. They went, in their thousands. Many being artisans moved as a community and happened to settle in the Berlin area. Over centuries, the Huguenot influence turned Berlin into the cultural centre of Europe by the late 1700s.

I scanned the lists of names of Huguenot families expecting to find the name Villeneuve, but to no avail. This left my family back in France. A new theory developed in my mind.

Artisans needed to attract the business from aristocrats in order to earn a good wage. That's where the money was and that is what the Huguenots did. Berlin was the capital of Prussia and Prussians held themselves in high esteem. They were the aristocracy. They were the clients of the Huguenots.

Meanwhile, back in France when the French revolution broke out in the late 1700s and the guillotine was being set up in the market square to deal with the French aristocrats, this became a nervous time for the artisans. Firstly they were losing business, but, more importantly, they might have been identified as being too close to the aristocracy for comfort. Their heads, too, might roll. [History had it that the site for the guillotine was the Place de la Révolution (now Place de la Concorde). It was said that it reeked so strongly of blood that even animals feared to enter the area]

Theodore's grandfather made the 'executive decision' to move the family east into Germany. "Why not to Berlin, the cultural centre of Europe?" He made a second executive decision, once there, to decree that only French would be spoken in the home. They must keep the French culture alive.

Before the close of the eighteenth century Theodore's father was born. Like his father before him, he became a jeweler and in 1822 Theodore was born. He too followed family tradition. By the time Theodore was in his early twenties he became concerned that now Prussia was beginning to "harass" the Huguenot communities. Though their own family was not Huguenot, the French name Villeneuve would likely get linked, for better or worse.

Theodore was restless and became more so as he heard of the excitement in London over the forthcoming Great Exhibition and World's Fair set to open in 1851. The 'Crystal Palace''', a state-of-the-art engineering masterpiece, featured almost 19 acres under one roof. The building that was 'portable', was being erected in Hyde Park to house the event.[2] Once the exhibition was over it would be disassembled and re-built in Sydenham in the country East of London. London itself was booming. Excitement was at a fever-pitch over there. This looked like a great opportunity.

Footnotes

1 Donald Combe, 'team member' – see 'Acknowledgments'.
2 *'To Engineer is Human'*, Chapter 12, The Crystal Palace, Henry Petroski, Professor of Civil Engineering, Duke University. Published by Vintage Books, a division of Random House, Inc., New York.

6

The One Way Trek

BERLIN – August 25, 1850

In the last week of August, Theodore was ready to start his trek across Europe. His worldly possessions in his back-pack and his stick (weapon) in hand, he waved farewell to his family and headed for Paris, his target location for the winter. There were over 1,000 kilometers of countryside between Berlin and Paris. He expected to cover this in four to six weeks. A target of 33 kilometers a day would put him in Paris the first week of October.

He had recognized that this was not a low risk undertaking and had planned accordingly. For safety he decided to take his dog Bruno, a black and tan Alsatian, who he had owned for more than three years. Bruno was trained to protect his master or his master's property. He was trained to respond to the word 'attack', though there had never been the occasion to see what happened in practice (a bit of risk there!). In theory, Bruno would cease to attack upon a whistle command from his master (this seemed to work).

Theo decided to add a second dog, a specialist in hunting. He had gone to the dog-pound and selected a friendly black retriever named Aggie. In a few trial trips to the open country, Theo had found Aggie a very enthusiastic hunter of small game and even the odd 'sitting duck'.

This looked after protection and food. Europe between Berlin and Paris was mostly lush countryside. Water was not expected to be a problem. Streams and rivers would be quite plentiful. Furthermore rain was not uncommon at any time. The biggest risk would probably be the possibility of an accident en-route. Two pairs of strong leather high-laced boots would reduce the risk of sprained or broken ankles. There were no mountain ranges to cross, no deserts; it is a matter of being careful.

At the last minute, Theo decided to take a heavy stick and a couple of holstered hunting knives. Theodore was fit with a strong lean athletic body. He seemed to be ready. "Oh! Mustn't forget the compass and maps." A magnifying glass for starting fires in sunny weather might help. His course would be to head South-West, through Frankfurt and Luxembourg, to Paris; a distance, 'as the crow flies', of about 1,000 kilometers.

The time had come to say goodbye to his parents. This would be hard since he was planning to settle in England and may never see them again. He decided not to stress the "never see them again" scenario. Trying to keep a cheerful farewell, he gave them both a hug and was on his way before any one of them, including himself, broke down.

En route, he expected to mainly live off the land, sleep under the stars in good weather, or sneak into an old barn to shelter in bad weather.

Theodore had also planned ahead. He had a contact in the jewelry trade in Paris who knew he was coming. Theodore was confident that he would find full-time employment for the winter. He was very good at his craft and could play a humble 'second fiddle' when needed. Late August and September were usually ideal months for travel weather-wise. His spirits were very high.

From time to time, there were ruffians lurking along the way who didn't even make a move when they spotted Bruno and Theo's heavy stick.

They were almost halfway without notable incident as they headed, South of Kessel, into a heavily wooded area, mostly aged oak trees. The sun had been almost relentless for the past few days and the leafy canopy and the rustle of leaves under foot were a pleasant change. The route was well marked by ruts from cart and coach wheels. Even so there was hardly a soul around moving in either direction. In some areas, even though it was near noon, the foliage was so thick that it was almost dark. As they entered one such area, suddenly five ruffians dropped out of the trees instantly surrounding Theo and the dogs....they were ambushed.

Bruno immediately assumed an attack stance, but waited for Theo's command. Theo waited to see what move the group would make. He drew his knife and gripped his stick in readiness. The ruffians also had knives and exchanged jokes and taunted Theo to act first. Theo had the dogs on leashes that consisted of a leather strap (no buckles) that was passed through the dog-harness and which he held at both ends. So without making a move he opened his fingers and dropped one end of Bruno's leash, shouting "ATTACK". Like lightning, Bruno streaked forward and in three bounds took the ringleader at chest level. He went down instantly. Bruno positioned himself with front paws above the ruffian's shoulders, haunches on his chest. Bruno's jaws closed on the ruffian's neck as he started shaking the man's head back and forth like a rabbit. In a moment the man lay motionless, his jugular artery ripped as the lifeblood gushed out soaking into the mossy earth. It was all over in a few seconds.

The other four ruffians panicked and started running. Theo whistled the command to Bruno who immediately ceased the attack and returned to Theo's side. One death was enough.

Now Theo dropped the one half of Aggie's leash so she bounded off after one of the ruffians, then spotting another and changing course. She wasn't quite sure what she had to do and she ended up not catching any of them. This was just as well. Had she caught one she might have licked him to death. Aggie, however, stopped running, looking pleased with herself. She was taking all the credit for chasing the ruffians away. Immediately she started poking around in the undergrowth and moments later, tail wagging, she approached Theo and Bruno with a rabbit for their lunch.

Theo did his best to cover up the corpse of the leader, using leaves and underbrush. He uttered a brief prayer asking for forgiveness for the cause of a death. He had no tools for digging a grave. It would not be long before the wildlife of the forest would devour the poor fellow.

Moving away from the site, Theo looked at his beloved dogs and decided that it was time for lunch. He built a fire, skinned the rabbit and prepared enough for all three of them.

As they were about to leave, Theo looked over to the site of Bruno's attack. Already the crows were circling, some landing on the body, setting about their ghoulish task of preparing their own lunch. Theo shivered. "There, but for the grace of God, go I."

Whether or not there was an 'underground telegraph' or 'grapevine' operating in the underworld of the forests, Theo didn't know. Nevertheless, there were no more problems on the road.

As Theo, Bruno and Aggie passed over the border and entered France, he was very thankful that his family had elected to maintain the French language all these years. There was, in fact, no indication that Theo was a foreigner. He just melted into the surroundings. The dogs, fortunately, were bi-lingual anyway.

On October 7, just about on schedule, the trio marched into Paris. They immediately made their way to the jeweler at 32 Boulevard St. Germain in the heart of the city to meet Theo's contact face-to-face for the first time. His name was Charles Lamond. Good to his word, Charles had a job lined up for Theo with another jeweler, George Riki, a few meters up the street. There Theo could ply his trade for ten hours a day, five days a week. Charles could also keep Theo busy weekends.

Charles had a small room in the back of his shop complete with a bed, of sorts, that he offered to Theo, Bruno and Aggie. When Theo thanked him profusely for all he was doing, Charles shrugged a shoulder and smiled shyly.

This was just what Theo wanted. His sole objective was to build up enough money to fund his first few weeks once he reached London. He would 'keep his head down' and avoid the social scene as much as possible in spite of the seductive charms that Paris could offer. In the evenings he had to study this exceedingly difficult language – English!

The one luxury Theo allowed himself was to take a short break mid-morning for coffee at the cafe next door. He would buy a copy of 'La Presse' and read about the excitement that was building up in London over the Great Exhibition of 1851. Yes he was sure there were opportunities ahead.

The weeks passed quickly. As soon as the Christmas celebrations were over Theo started to look into the requirements for emigration from France and immigration into England. He already knew that he would be sailing from Le Havre for Southampton. One final thing was to talk to the bank about transferring his savings to London. With this much money, he didn't want to carry it or he would be worth robbing now. Even Bruno had his dissuasive limits! (or did he?).

It turned out that artisans were much sought-after in Britain, especially now, with the exhibition and all. Formalities were quite minimal for humans. Dogs had to travel in cages stowed in the hold. Banking was simpler than he expected. Everything seemed to be ready. Another month and the daffodils and crocuses would be out in the London parks by the time they arrived.

7

Landfall 1851

I first saw her by the rail, looking through the light mist towards the distant English coast. But there were so many people on the ship that it was hard to get any closer. She was tall and elegant, out of place among the mix of immigrants, French, Spanish, Italian, Dutch and German. She had such a regal poise; she could not have been missed.

She then turned slowly, supporting her back against the rail as she talked quietly to her companion, a somewhat older lady. I tried not to stare at her and I lowered my head for a moment. When I next looked up, her head was turning quickly away from my direction as if she might intuitively have felt my stare.

Moments later I spotted one of her gloves lying on the deck. I manoeuvred my way slowly through the crowd, trying to be as unobtrusive as possible until I was beside her as I bent down and retrieved it.

"Pardon Mademoiselle, I believe this is your glove?"

She took the glove then looked at me and with a

slight smile.

"Thank you Monsieur."

She had accepted her 'single' status and had assumed that I was French. But where do we go from here? She turned again and gazed at the approaching landscape. I did the same and we remained silent for a while. I finally broke the silence.

"You have visited England before?"

"No, this is my first time."

Her voice had a pleasant middle-tone pitch. I detected an accent, but from where? To test her reaction I said: "It is my first visit too and I hope to remain here, I see great potential".

"In what way Monsieur?"

"Business career, that sort of thing."

"Then what do you do?"

"I am a goldsmith. I hope to build my own company here."

"How does one *become* a goldsmith?" Again she smiled and a slight challenge was in her eyes, thinking she had caught me trying to impress her.

"For me, Mademoiselle, it helps, coming from a family of goldsmiths who have been in the jewelry trade for many, many years."

"Oh!" She paused. "So where does your family live?"

"Berlin."

"BERLIN?" she repeated with surprise.

"Yes but only for the last seventy years," I said with mock apology. "Before that we were in Paris. Our name is Villeneuve. We walked out on the French revolution."

"A Villeneuve in Berlin would be assumed to be a Huguenot. You are not a Huguenot?"

There was something rather hilarious about being 'notahuguenot'. We both saw the funny side of this. We really laughed. We had somehow magically transcended the polite measured response. This was our first honest giggle. I switched to German.

"So tell me, how do you know about the Huguenots in Berlin?"

"I am Prussian. Our family name is Von Borne. We were not far from Berlin. We were often ... back and forth," she replied rather vaguely.

I found it charming how she eked out bits of information always leaving a veil of mystery to 'hang in the air' when she finished.

The rhythmic throb of the ships steam-engine suddenly changed and the sails were being furled. While we had been talking we had not noticed that we were slipping into the protection of the Isle of Wight as we approached Southampton. It will not be long before we are herded into different lines as our papers are examined. There were precious minutes left to make sure she didn't escape. I said:

"We are almost there and we haven't yet been introduced. I understand that the British are very formal on these matters."

"You should have met my family," she laughed, "they were even more so." (The past tense was left 'floating' with no explanation.)

With a little mock-ceremony I delved into my wallet and produced 'my card' with a flourish and solemnly handed it to her as I gave a formal bow, simultaneously clicking my heels.

"Mademoiselle, please accept my credentials. My address is of course already out of date and it may be a few days before I have a London address. How may I reach you?"

"I will be in Bloomsbury with my aunt." And with this she shyly handed me her calling card. Handwritten on her aunt's card was her own name 'Johanna'.

I tucked the card in my wallet. *She cannot escape me now!*

8

The Villeneuve Beachhead

As expected, Johanna and Theodore did get separated in the confusion of disembarkation. In his master-plan he had expected to be highly focused on his next moves. He suddenly realized that he was far from it. He simply felt confused and somewhat shaken by the last few hours. His mind was obsessed by the thought of Johanna. "Good God," he thought, "I might be in love." This was a totally new experience.

The journey up to London took considerably longer that the trip from France to Britain. This slow progress seemed to calm Theo down. He had time to think. He was in charge. He had the 'key' to seeing Johanna again. That was all that mattered. He must get settled first and the sooner the better.

His master-plan that was gradually coming back into focus, reminding Theo that he needed to concentrate on establishing himself in the Clerkenwell district of London. This was the heart of the gold, silver and jewelry trade. What he needed to do was find a place to stay and get a job within the trade he was qualified.

Within a day he had found an inexpensive one-room accommodation. (Pay in advance for two weeks at a time.) He now had a London address – 45 Compton Street, Clerkenwell.

For the next two days, Theodore walked the streets of Clerkenwell, gradually building up a picture of the various goldsmiths and jewelers in the area. Encouragingly, he found that Northampton Square, only two blocks north of Compton Street, seemed to be the focal point. This small square had no less than five jewelry establishments. If only he could find work in this square he felt this was *the* place to be. One day he might even own his own business right here.

When he next looked, he found that three out of the five businesses had their sign 'so-and-so & son' (or 'sons' or 'brothers'). Unless they were really busy, a job with one of these 'family businesses' was unlikely. Let's start with the other two. For some reason, when he viewed the outside of number 28 he got a good feeling. The name was simply 'Appleby – GOLD',

Theo had spent the winter in Paris attending evening classes that taught 'conversational English'. Now was the time to test the progress he had

Number 28 Northampton Sq. Clerkenwell London EC1 (as it stands today)

Photo
Donald Combe
January 2006

made in this third language. He plucked up courage.

LONDON – February 2, 1851. 3 p.m. It was raining.

Theodore walked into the shop. It was more a workshop than a store and there at a bench an elderly grey-haired man was buffing a gold item. He looked up rather impatiently. "Yes?"

"Pardon me Sir, would you be Mr. Appleby, the owner?"

"Do I look like a figure of fun?" he growled.

"Indeed not, Sir". Theo thought this sounded like pretty good English. Those more familiar with the

English language might have interpreted this as "No, you look like a miserable bugger". Fortunately Appleby took the remark at face value and just shrugged.

"You have to see I am terribly busy. Mostly stuff with a deadline for this 'Great Exhibition' that Prince Albert got launched last year. I haven't had a decent nights' sleep since. So what do you want?"

"I have just arrived from Paris where I was working for George Riki on Boulevard St Germain. Have you, perhaps heard of him, Sir?"

"No".

"My name is Theodore Villeneuve. My family has been goldsmiths for many, many years. Their business is in Berlin."

"BERLIN – are you one of them Huguenot fella's they talk about?"

"No, I am not a Huguenot." Suddenly Johanna's beautiful animated face flashed before him, her laughter filled his ears, as they shared this inside joke only a few days earlier. He struggled to keep a straight face. (Declaring oneself to be "notahuguenot" followed by a guffaw or even an idiotic grin would be the 'kiss of death' to any interview!) Miraculously he survived this moment.

"Then how come the fancy French name?"

Theo explained that his family moved out of France 70 years ago to avoid the threat of the guillotine. (Damn, now he'll think the Villeneuves were aristocracy. He wanted to steer the interview back to his need of a job.) Theo cringed, waiting for the next one-liner salvo from Appleby.

"Oh well then! So you be one of them

h'aristocrats."

"No Sir, I am not". (Is this man a professor of history, or what?) "It was just that the artisans worked for the aristocrats and the tribunals judged the artisans to be too close to them. A few lost their heads."

Theo noticed a twinkle in Appleby's eye. The old man had been teasing him. Appleby now let him off the hook. "So, what makes you think you can be of help to me, lad?"

"I apprenticed in the family firm starting at age 12. I have 10 years of experience as a qualified goldsmith." As he was speaking, he pulled an envelope from his inside pocket and laid it on the counter. "These are my credentials. I am good at what I do." He paused "Sir, I don't want to be impertinent, but I believe that since you are so busy with deadline work, I could ease your burden by taking over the more menial tasks and leaving you free to concentrate on the creative aspects."

Appleby slumped back in his chair. He looked completely exhausted. He took a deep breath and then let it out slowly in a long sigh.

"I hear what you say, lad. Leave your papers. I'll look at them. Come back in two days after I have given this some thought. Don't expect anything permanent though. If I might offer anything at all, it will only be on a trial basis. Now, be on your way, I have to get on with things."

"Thank you Sir, I appreciate that you have been so generous with your time." He said this sincerely. He had no thought to be sarcastic. He liked the old man.

Theo was back out in the rain in all of five minutes!

Theodore walked away from Northampton Square with a positive feeling about the interview. His first thought was to write a note to Johanna to tell her the news, but he then decided to wait until he had actually been hired. He should know one way or the other in two days.

So for the next two days, Theo expanded his exploration of Clerkenwell. When he spotted a library he went in to find a street map of London and to see if he could find 'Bloomsbury'. He was surprised how huge London was, but when he found The District of Bloomsbury, he was pleased to see that it was the next district West of Clerkenwell.

He pulled out Johanna's card. She was with the aunt who lived at 32 Russell Square. Good heavens, this was almost next door to the British Museum, probably only a 20-minute walk from here. The temptation was to go there straight away. But no, he didn't want to be seen lurking around her neighborhood and one cannot just knock on the door and turn up uninvited.

Theo contented himself with scanning the map to familiarize himself with the landmarks and parks that he and Johanna would be able to explore.

Within easy walking distance there to the South-East was the Tower of London. One could follow the river upstream from there to Westminster. Or if one went directly West from Russell Square, there was Regents Park. But then there were St. James's

Park and Green Park, all around the Buckingham Palace area. One could easily reach Hyde Park where the 'Great Exhibition of 1851' is to be held. Just walk down Oxford Street to Hyde Park Corner, then walk South-East through the park towards Knightsbridge (you can't miss it). Now that's where we will be going on May 1 when the Queen will be opening the Exhibition. We will walk into the Crystal Palace. (Just think! A year from now, this huge building will be taken down and moved to Sydenham, East of London. What an engineering triumph!)[1]

Theodore entered Appleby's shop, just 48 hours after his first interview. The scene looked almost identical to the last time. Old Appleby was still buffing what looked like the same piece. He looked up from his work, just like last time. But this time he was less gruff. "Ah! Mr. Villeneuve! Come in."

"I have decided to give you a try. You have to understand that one never knows how people will get on, how they will work together day after day. I am giving you a try since you have experience and seem to be of an honest disposition. I will simply have to review the situation at the end of each week and my decision will be final. I will expect you to work from 8 a.m. till 6 p.m. Monday to Friday and 8 a.m. till 12 noon on Saturday. I will pay you 8 shillings a week. If you are agreeable to this I will see you tomorrow morning at 8 a.m. sharp".

Appleby handed Theodore back his papers.

"I agree. 8 a.m. sharp! Thank you Sir".

Theodore was pleased. He had achieved a beachhead at his prime location within his first week in London. The money was not that great but this could be negotiated upward when he had proved his value to Appleby.

Unbeknown to Theodore, Appleby was feeling relieved and mildly elated that he might finally have managed to get knowledgeable help that he so desperately needed. Unlike nearly all the jewelers in business who had sons or brothers to draw on, Appleby had none. He had simply arrived at old age with no family to speak of, only one antagonistic brother with whom there had been no communication for years now.

Appleby needed to slow down before his health completely unraveled. He needed someone he could rely on to take over. Of course it would be months before he would know for sure. His own attitude would have to change. In the past, he had fired a few helpers, but a larger number had 'fired' him and simply stormed out. This had got to change.

Appleby had a scenario of his own. If and when the time arrived that he and Villeneuve could tolerate and trust each other he would next see if Villeneuve would move to the upper floor over the shop. He had lived up there himself until his rheumatism got so bad that he couldn't climb the stairs. He couldn't even use it for storage since it would be unreachable to him. To have someone on the premises that had the ability and knowledge to take charge when necessary would be a huge load off Appleby's mind.

As for Theodore, he had to get a letter to Johanna

as quickly as possible telling her the good news, and to set up their first date. He had better get some calling cards printed now that he had a London address.

Theo had a day or so to think and to turn his attention to his beloved dogs. Bruno appeared to be settling down to city life; but Aggie was clearly not. She was a country-lover and that is where her skills lay. Early one morning, Theo took Aggie for a walk. They headed for Covent Garden Market. Here, at dawn, the farmers came into town with their carts full of crops for sale. Even the smell of this gathering got Aggie's tail wagging again. Theo walked around looking for the candidate who might like to take over Aggie. Soon he spotted a farmer, clearly a family man who had his children with him. There was laughter in their area along with the business of moving the produce. Theo engaged the farmer in conversation and explained the *plight* of his dear Aggie and offered her at no cost. The farmer, Jim Philpot, signaled the children in to come closer and meet Aggie.

It was lover at first sight. Everyone was a winner. Theo, as he started to break down at the thought of losing Aggie was assured that she would be part of the Covent Garden scene from now on. They would all be expecting Theo to visit at least once a week. Theo responded by having Bruno join him on the visits.

It transpired that as Theo settled down in his

job under Appleby, he and Johanna started to see each other on every possible occasion. In practical terms, Saturday afternoon and Sunday were the only possible times and, of course, one had to accommodate church. Johanna had a bright idea:

"Theo, since we belong to no specific church, why don't we visit a different church each week. I have been reading about Christopher Wren. I would love to visit all the churches that he designed and built after the Great Fire of London. There are dozens of them surrounding St. Paul's, his master-work."

"Great idea," said Theo. "If we brought along sandwiches or a picnic lunch, we could head right out after the service to the parks." Johanna was a bit shocked. "Do you really think we could do that?" "I don't see why not, so long as we didn't start eating them during the sermon, and so long as their delicious fragrance does not make the congregation too hungry to sit through to the end!"

"That's why I love you Theo; you always see the light side. You can always make me laugh."

This may have been the start of Theo's interest in architecture and why he was, later in life, to take his young grandson Percy Hale on architectural tours through the city.

Within 5 months following the fateful meeting between Theo and Johanna as their ship approached England, they were married. Theo had no family in England while Johanna only had her one aunt,

The steeples of the Wren churches in London 1851

thus the wedding was a small affair. They selected their favourite Wren church, Saint Brides, which stands at the bottom of Ludgate Hill where it becomes Fleet Street. The steeple is famous for its extravagant carvings and became known as the 'Wedding Cake Steeple'.

A few days before the wedding, Theo took Johanna to the shop to meet old Appleby and tell him the news. For all his gruff exterior, he could be very charming, especially before such a beautiful young woman. On the spur of the moment he made an uncharacteristic snap decision. He offered the couple the upper two floors of number 28, rent-free, as a wedding present and part of Theo's raise in compensation. *"They cannot escape me now,"* he thought.

The Vicar carried out the ceremony to an empty church with only the bridal couple, Johanna's aunt and the Vicar's wife as witnesses. The honeymoon started on July 29, 1851 at number 28 Northampton Square, Clerkenwell.

There is a mix of fact and fiction once again. It is fact that Theodore and Johanna did move in to the upper floor at 28 Northampton Square. (They decided to speak only German in the house which made sense perfect to Theodore since his own family insisted they spoke only French in the house when he was living in Germany.) In that first year together they visited the Crystal Palace and many of the London parks. It is a fact that as the years passed, they had a total of six children[3] who all spoke English with a German accent. It is a fact that the youngest, Albert, spent most of his career in Poland where he taught English, so he also spoke Polish. It is possible that generations of his students unknowingly mastered the English language as spoken with a German accent!

It is fact that Theo's eldest daughter, Isabella, was my grandmother and that she married Edward Hale. They had one son, Percy Edward Hale, my father. He spoke only English! Percy was the only known grandchild of Theodore! He became an architect and a great admirer of Sir Christopher Wren. It is a fact that Percy, during the 1930s, took *his* son Neville, on architectural tours of 'the City' before the London Blitz of 1940 destroyed a majority of the Wren churches ... but not St Brides at the foot of Ludgate Hill...

One has to fictionalize that Theodore worked well with the fictional Appleby and in due course Theo took over the business. It is fact that he appears listed in the Business Directory of London, 1884, (classified section – Gold) as 'Villeneuve, Theodore, 28 Northampton Square, Clerkenwell'.

Footnotes

1 'To Engineer is Human', Chapter 12 , 'Interlude – The Success Story of the Crystal Palace', Henry Petroski, First Vintage Books Edition, April 1992, a Division of Random House, Inc., New York.

2 Queen Victoria visited [the exhibition] no less than 50 times between May 1 and October 15, 1851. She seemed never to tire of spending hours methodically touring the exhibits. A retrospective entry from the Queen's journal for the closing day reads: "To think that this great and bright time is past, like a dream, after all its success and triumphs".

3 Theodore and Johanna's children. **Theodore Louis**: Born Dec. 1852. Left for Australia as a young man (before 1881 census) losing touch with the family. **Isabella, Henrietta, Susanah**: Born 1857. Married Edward Hale 1886. Died 1940. **Frederich**: Born 1859. Listed as jeweler in 1891 census, dropped out of society and became a vagrant, death unknown. **Minnie**: Born 1863 had left home by 1881 Census and worked as a servant for another household. **Louise**: Born 1864. Had left home prior to 1891 census and worked as a servant for another household. **Albert**:

Born 1869 became a scholar and teacher of English and taught in Poland for most of his life. Died in Poland 1938.

From this whole family there was only one grandchild for Theodore and Johanna – **Percy Edward Hale**, A.R.I.B.A. Born 1887. Married Violet Johnson, 1919. Died 1954. Percy had a daughter, **Moyra (Molly)**, and a son, **Neville Edward**. Neville married and inherited stepchildren but no children of his own. Molly was a war-bride and married Canadian Dr. Robert Bigelow. This kept the Villeneuve bloodline going through three boys, grandchildren and great grandchildren.

9

Looking Good

She stands, in all her beauty, 56 cm in height on a circular base 3 cm thick. She is a Galvano Plastique (bronze-over-plaster), treated with a black patina. She is pristine after 120 years within the Villeneuve-Hale family.

So much for statistics! It is personality that counts. Take a look at the little figure. Put a baton in her hand and she will start strutting, leading a marching band. Look again and she sways to the swirling music of Jule Styne's *'Dancing in the Dark'* or Cole Porter's *'You are so Easy to Love'*.

Go for an extreme close-up and she is ageless, from Egypt perhaps, or from Ancient Greece. Perhaps only from Paris in 1884.[5]

As custodian of this lovely creature for the past 50 years, I have recently been asking persons who view her for the first time: "How old do you think she is?"

On one occasion, a lady who had heard quite a lot about my research and writings on the Black Statue and now seeing her for the first time, turned to me and said accusingly: "But she is only a child. I was never told that! She could only be 10 years old". She only had to point and I knew that her conclusion was based on one parameter only … no visible sign of breasts. Not knowing the lady that well, I was simply was too shy to launch into my theory about body-dynamics under extreme poses. My point, however, can be upheld simply from viewing photos of the ballet dancer in full-flight while performing the *grande jeté*, or the pair-skaters where the girl is held aloft on one upraised arm of her partner as she assumes a *flying spiral* attitude. In these kinds of situations the small breasted athletic body stretches out to assume, what my mother always tactfully referred to as *"a boyish figure"*.

As a matter of fact I am sufficiently old, yet young enough, to remember my observations as a child and young teenager in the late 1920's and early 30s. This was the time of the Flappers, the young 'in' crowd who danced wildly to the Charleston. Lithesome young girls and women (including my sister) stayed in great shape this way as they strived to achieve the much admired "boyish figure". Old movies of the 1920s era tell the same story. This was the fashion. Breasts were *out* until the mid thirties, *when Hollywood decided it was time for a change.*

There have been other reactions too ...

Neighbours of mine run an antique business that focuses on Art Deco restoration. I was anxious to show them the Black Statue, expecting and receiving helpful comments to include in my book. I was invited to dinner and saw their living quarters for the first time. For me it was like a time warp to my childhood days. My Black Statue, though created fifty years before *that* time, looked completely *at home* in these beautiful Art Deco surroundings. As we sat at dinner, the Black Statue stood on the table bathed in soft lighting. Conversation revolved around her.

After dessert, I popped the question "How old

do you think she is?". My host reached out and slowly rotated her through a full circle. The answer came immediately. "Seventeen." I hinted about "the boyish figure". This was waved off impatiently. "Look at the hip development. This is a beautiful young woman."

This was a good number. It was the age of Camille Claudel, the talented young sculptor, when she arrived in Paris in 1881. By age 19 she was employed by Rodin as an apprentice sculptor. She also started modeling for him (exclusively) for works that remain world famous to this day. Her participation included 'The Kiss', 'Danaid', 'Eternal Idol', 'Kneeling Faun' and 'Erect Faun'. These last two were for the famous, never completed, 'Gates of Hell'. (They were later detached by Rodin, to have "lives of their own".)

In any event, one must keep in mind that there is sometimes a difference between reality and the artist's interpretation of what he/she sees. It is on record that Rodin chose to present busts (portraits) of Camille as *"being childlike"*. There was no reason given for this biographic statement, yet this seems to be the case for the Black Statue. If Rodin favoured the *childlike face*[5] it is highly unlikely that he would present the childlike face on a mature figure!

Hands, for Rodin, *expressed the quintessence of his art.* They were the fragments that stood for the whole. "Having *got them right*" meant, to Rodin, that he now felt confident in his power.[1]

The fact that he, Rodin, entrusted "getting them right" to Camille showed the enormous faith he had in her skill and ability. She then held "the

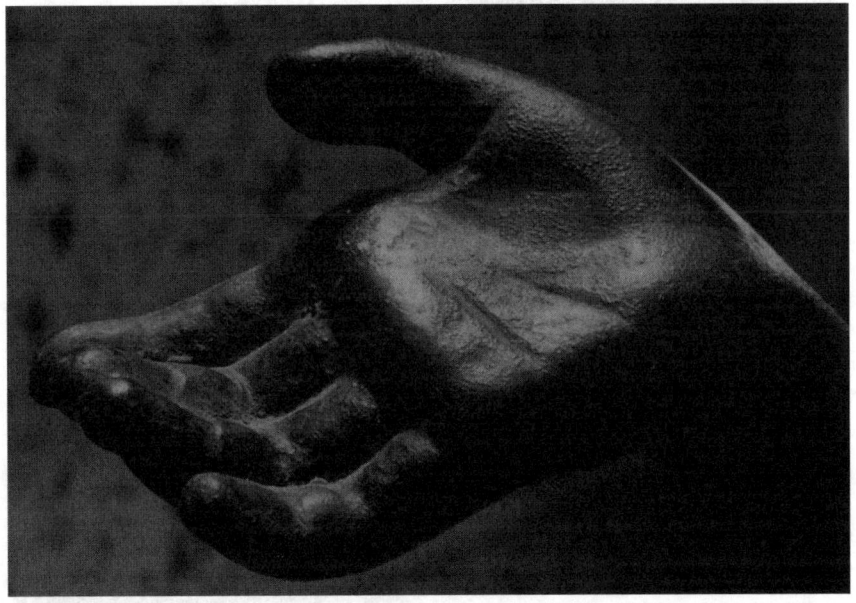

power" in her hands. She had the power to set the mood.

Author/writer Edmond de Goncourt, a friend and critic of Rodin's work, had this to say: *"Rodin excels in the modeling of the curve of the back and as it were, the beating wings of their shoulders".*[2]

Sarah Milroy added: "His work has *a sense of pent-up physicality and sensuality for which Rodin is justly famous".*[3]

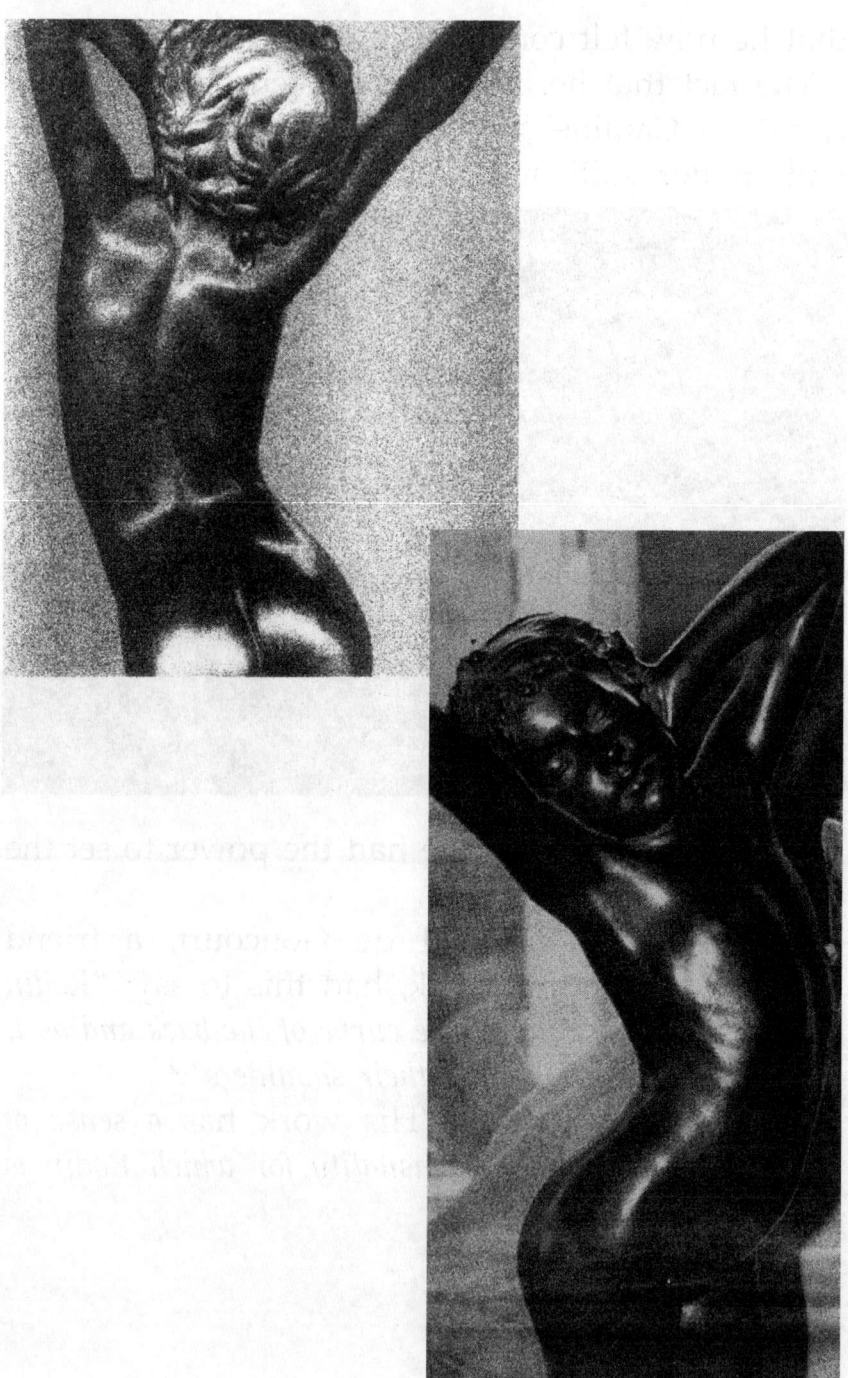

References

1 *'RODIN. A Biography'*, Frederic Grunfeld, page 214 (hands).
2 *'RODIN. A Biography'*, Frederic Grunfeld, page 257 (curve of back).
3 Sarah Milroy, *Globe & Mail* (national newspaper Toronto), *'RODIN – truly a bust'*, September 22, 2001.
4 http://www.cs.wustl.edu/~loui/camille.html_page 3.
5 http://www.dia.org/exhibitions/claudel_rodin/preview2.asp ... 'TETE-A-TETE'
Camille depicted as « *childlike with an enigmatic expression ... the impression of a strong personality and yet traces of youthful fragility are expressed in these portraits...* » [by Rodin in early works with Camille as model].

10

Secrets Within

This story has a number of facets that run more or less in parallel, some concluding earlier and some later in time. I therefore go back to September 22, 2001, when my interest was first aroused. The question "what if?" first came to mind.

The very first act of investigation was to peel back the green baize material on the underside of the base. Immediately there was a surprise. In the centre of the base there was a rugged, randomly shaped cavity, about 3 x 4 cm in size. Through this one could look into the statue to the depth of about 4 cm, and view the 'whitish' modeling material.

Because of the known age (in 2005) at 120 years, it was like looking into a newly opened time capsule. The underside of the base had the same black patina that treated the whole statue. But here it was sparser and it was contaminated by the adhesive from the baize pad just removed. A few abrasions showed glints of bronze in spots through the base.

I looked carefully for a signature, or any type of identity stamp. There were none.

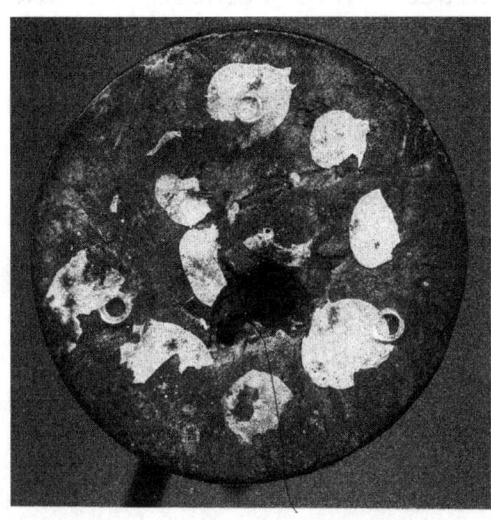

Underside of Base – Computer scan (Plastic rings to protect scan-glass. White patches of adhesive following removal of base pad.)

Projecting slightly proud of the plaster, one could see and touch a piece of metal rod, believed to be brass and about 5 mm diameter. It wasn't the end of the rod, but more like a portion of a right-angle bend or hook shape. It seemed logical at the time that it should be the bottom of a strengthening member that would run up through the body and into the raised right arm, which was clearly the most vulnerable part of the work.

There was a very early and limited assumption, mainly based on the ragged cavity and the presence of an armature, that the statue *might be* an original rather than be one of a multiple reproduction run, enough conviction to *keep the flame burning.*

It was almost three years later, in August 2004 (and just after I had met with sculptor Dale Dunning – Chapter 1), that I plucked up courage and attempted to extract small samples of the modeling compound for examination.

At my first attempt I took a 1/8" drill, selected a spot near the cavity and drilled in to a depth of about 8 mm. It was my expectation that the modeling material of such age would come out as powder. It did not. The modeling material remained stuck in the drill flutes, seemed slightly sticky and was, in part, a yellow-ochre colour. I thought it might be bees-wax. I was able to flake out the material from the drill and obtain three tiny samples.

I selected one and put a blow-lamp on it, raising it to a red glow. When I removed the blow-lamp, a small flame continued to flicker for a few seconds finally leaving a few grains of a white gritty substance that was incombustible. I repeated this on a second sample with a similar result. I didn't have the facilities or the knowledge to go any further on my own.

One of my team members, Nancy Green, used to work for The Canadian Conservation Institute (C.C.I.). She provided the connections for me. This is a Federal Government division of 'Canadian Heritage'. Their primary expertise lies in analysis of paintings, forgery investigations and so forth. When

I first opened discussions with them they indicated that they had not been involved in statuary to any great extent, but were keen to do so.

I negotiated a small contract with C.C.I. to analyze a sample for me. A formal contract was drawn up. A statement of work was provided to me indicating the method of analysis.

The work would include x-ray microanalysis, x-ray diffraction (XRD), Fourier transform infrared spectroscopy (FTIR) and polarizing light microscopy (PLM). The terms were set, the price was agreed and a sample was mailed to Ottawa on November 3, 2004.

The final report is dated April 17, 2005. The 'bottom line' indicated the interesting result that the 'modeling compound' consisted of 28% hydrocarbon wax "such as Paraffin wax" and 68% of some form of "chemically precipitated gypsum or hardened Plaster of Paris" (by weight). The report also informed that Plaster of Paris is made "by roasting native gypsum at 100–190 Deg. C. where it loses three-quarters of its 'water-of-crystallization' and becomes calcium sulphate hemihydrate". It was incredible to me that so much information could be obtained from such a small sample weighing, maybe, one gram!

To really understand all this, and bearing in mind that we are focused on Paris of 1880s, we looked up the name 'Plaster of Paris'. The origin appeared to come from the fact that the Montmartre district of Paris was the site of quarries containing a huge supply of gypsum.

To the Parisian sculptors of the 1880s, the material in the quarries of Montmartre was just a handy local source. It is probable that the sculptors converted this to plaster by roasting, as they needed it.

The name "Plaster of Paris" probably came into being when businessmen and industrialists started converting the gypsum to plaster on a grand scale and marketing it far and wide. plaster of Paris, when mixed with water in the ratio of 4 parts powder to 3 parts water, forms a solid material that does not shrink when it cures. It is ideal for producing castings from a female mould without loss of definition. This makes Plaster of Paris quite unique.

So what is the reason for the large content of wax?

If one is being guided by an expert in Galvano Plastique, or 'metallization of plaster' one would be told there would be the requirement to waterproof the plaster in order for the casting to withstand the electroplating bath without erosion.

A publication on electroplating dated 1930[1] described a waterproofing method for non-conductive materials such as plaster or wood. This was a dipping process into melted wax at a temperature of 125 deg. C. making sure that all air had bubbled out before removal.

This method, resulting in a thin surface layer of

wax, would not explain a 28% (by weight) content. One might say that the particular sample happened to be taken where the wax had congealed, and 28% was not representative to the whole statue. This might be so, except for the method of taking the sample. The sample was a 'core sample' which indicated that the wax must have been *integrated with the plaster at all depths, not just a surface coating.*

I decided to try to produce a casting of wax/ plaster combination comparable to the findings of C.C.I. I first cast a small disc (3" dia. by ½" thk.) using plaster of Paris/water mix as recommended by the supplier (Sample 1). I then boiled water and melted down paraffin wax candles to about a 3:1 water/wax mix. While still close to boiling I poured this water/wax into a mould then immediately added and stirred in the plaster of Paris to produce approximately the same mix as reported by C.C.I. Unexpectedly, the 'hot' process did not accelerate the curing time. On the contrary, *it slowed down the hardening process.* I later cut each of the samples into two halves (semi-circles) and soaked these in water for several days. Sample 1 did not deteriorate as much as I had expected, though it softened noticeably, whereas sample 2 appeared to be unchanged.

The most interesting observation was that the wax content of sample 2 resulted in a *much harder material* than the standard plaster cast, sample 1. *It was almost like marble!*

Had I, perhaps, stumbled on Danielli's 'malleable marble' formula, the material with no history of existence?

Having an 'inventor' background myself, I somehow started to think of Danielli as one who might have 'invented' a proprietary material (malleable marble) to create a product for promotion and sale. He might have done this when *the obvious*, dipping in wax, would be just as effective. I started to change my opinion after re-reading Sarah Milroy's comments about exhibits at the ROM in 2001, which seemed to lack *fine definition*. It was as if some sculptures had been dipped in a varnish that had congealed. To quote from her article: "*In plaster cast after plaster cast, the forms are blunted and abraded, sometimes as if dipped in a coating which has congealed over the surfaces, leaving the shapes generalized*".[2]

I started to think of Danielli as a highly sensitive and inventive individual. He had recognized that 'waterproofing' plaster by dipping it in hot wax would dramatically *blunt the forms, leaving the shapes generalized*. His sensitivity to this issue might have been brought about by his year in Greece studying ancient sculpture that gave breadth to his technical education.

Whatever the reason, he had come up with a brilliant solution to the waterproofing problem; the dry-mixing of plaster powder and powdered wax.

The fact that this resulted in a marble-like hardness may have been serendipity but is neither here or there, though he may have foreseen this too.

If the true 'work of art' is the 'studio plaster', *the closest to the artist's hand*, then the Galvano Plastique bronze sheath captures the master's work with no chance of losing definition. Galvano Plastique eliminates the extensive handling by foundry personnel beyond reach of the artist's control.

What Danielli was potentially doing was inventing an arguably better solution than the labour intensive 'lost wax' *foundry casting operations*, (the root of Sarah Milroy's criticism of many exhibits at the ROM). It seems that Danielli did not succeed in changing Rodin's course, once the experimental phase of Galvano Plastique came to an end at the Rodin studio. It is probable, though, that his work played a profound part in the art nouveau period that followed.

Footnotes

1 'Principles of Electroplating and Electroforming', Blum and Hogaboom, McGraw Hill 1930, 2nd Ed.
2 Sara Millroy, art critic, *Globe & Mail*, September 22, 2001.

11

X-ray Eyes

As I have indicated in 'Acknowledgments', Terry's input has been particularly vital since he has the determination to overpower my stubborn tendency to accept the obvious. This was never more important than the time when he kept insisting that we should get the statue x-rayed.

My defense was the fact that we know there is an armature. We can see a bit of it and even touch it through the cavity in the base. It is *obvious* that this rod is there to reinforce the extended right arm which is *obviously* the most vulnerable part of the statue. Terry would reply "We don't KNOW that! As always, I eventually gave in.

But where could I go for x-rays? Hospitals are far too busy. So are clinics. In any event, she would need an OHIP card to get in the door. This was impossible. I was so busy looking at impossible solutions that I didn't think of the obvious.

My son Jim is a veterinary surgeon in Campbellford, Ontario. I phoned him up and outlined what I needed. I explained that the statue was bronze plated over plaster. On hearing this, he was dubious and he thought that his equipment would not do the job. So he phoned Dr. Jim Bell who graduated with him back in the 70s and who was the vet in my town, Collingwood. He had a state-of-the-art x-ray facility. So after Jim had set up the introduction, I phoned Jim Bell and asked him when it would be convenient. "Come in at 2 o'clock today." It was October 8, 2004.

I had visualized doing this in off-hours. It turned out that the surgery was very busy. All these worried animal owners cuddling their pets. I walk in *with a statue*!!! The animals were discrete enough to pretend not to notice. The owners just kept staring. Then I was called in before everyone else. (*Obviously* an emergency.)

We got set-up and Jim said "We'll just have to guess at a setting and see what we get". The very first shot took in the upper body, arms and head. Moments later he emerged from the lead-lined x-ray room and moved to the printer. He pushed a button and slowly the life-size transparency started to emerge. Right away Jim said: "Looks like we got something". The exposure setting was perfect. He took two more shots and the whole statue was on X-ray film. The setting was 80,000 volts at 250 milliamps for 1/30th of a second.

The interpretation was to rage on for many weeks.

12

Hidden Beauty

With this new evidence before us, only one thing is obvious. We are looking at *a radical pose-modification to a previous statue.* (Is this an original studio product ... or what?)

Our own limited research into armatures indicates that for most artists 'anything goes' providing it produces the required strength. Our reference *'From Clay to Bronze – A Studio Guide to Figurative Sculpture'* by Tuck Langland[1] provides numerous illustrations of armatures which are crude, but do the job. Aesthetics appear unimportant since they will never see the light of day, they just provide reinforcement. The attached illustrations from the book make this point.

A BBC documentary in the 'Masterworks' series showed forensic work on Degas wax statue *'The Little Dancer'*. Degas found that the ferules from his old paint brushes made ideal props and braces for wire or pipe body-armatures. Nobody seemed to create 'beautiful' or 'elegant' armatures... what would be the point? It had to be practical and cheap.

Yet the armature in the raised arm is unusual in its beauty as a 'piece of wire-sculpture'. While being created, the artist already knew that it would be hidden forever. Why is this?

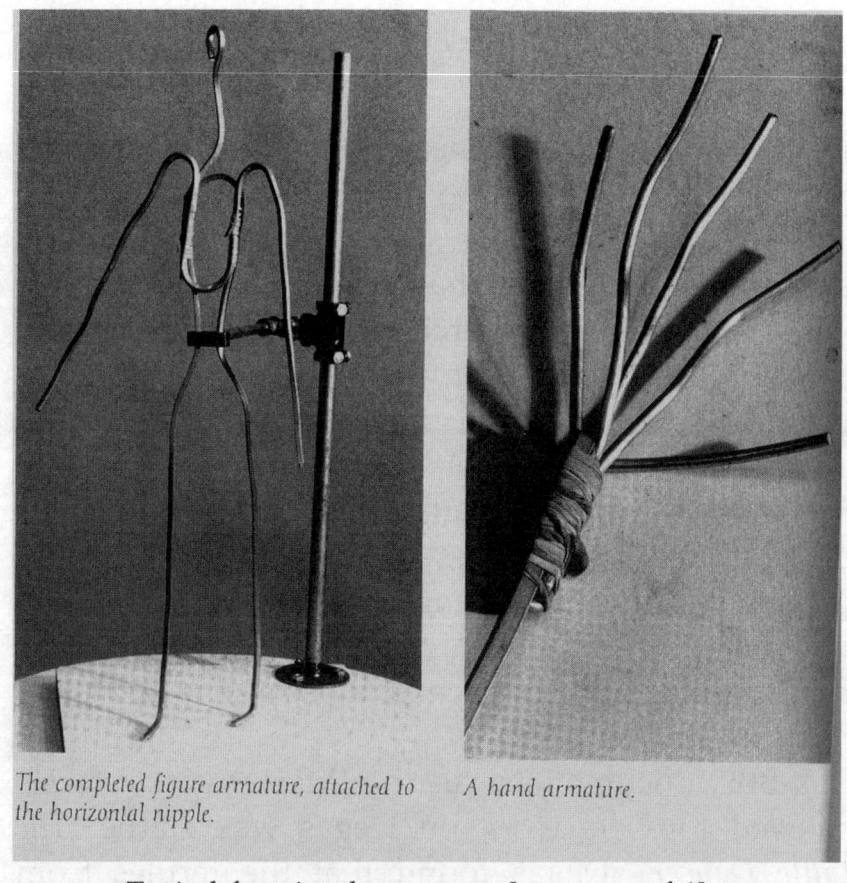

The completed figure armature, attached to the horizontal nipple.

A hand armature.

Typical functional armatures [courtesy ref 1]

So there has to be something really special about the armature that has been revealed in the Black Statue. Perhaps it is not so much the armature *per se* but the *personality of the creator*. This person must have been a highly driven perfectionist. There would be no glory for this little wire masterpiece. It was to be hidden for the next 120 years if not forever, yet it had to be perfect in the creator's eyes.

While a bar with a wire hand at the end secured by tape or piano-wire would have sufficed, this armature imitates nature in the sense that form is following function. Notice the upper arm has three-wire strength, the forearm one-wire strength and the wrist and hand use smaller wires running to the thumb, index finger and a third wire that strengthens the group of the three other fingers and the palm of the hand.

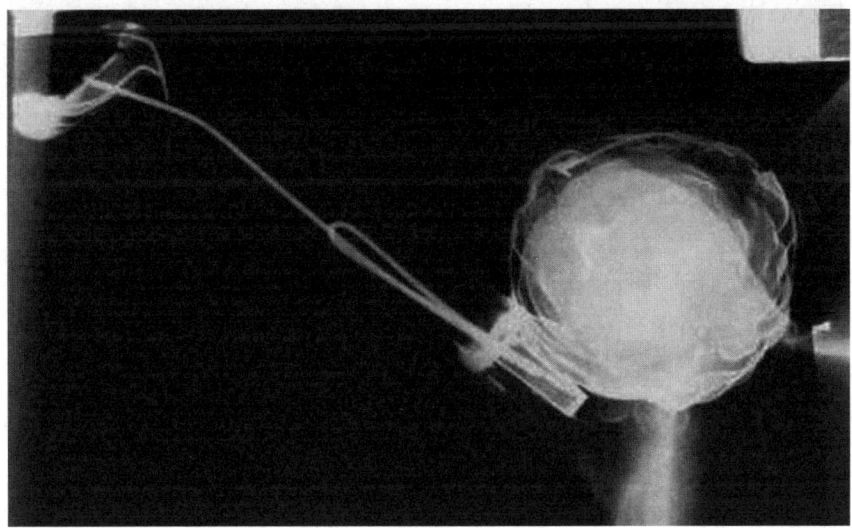

The elegance of the design stunned me … like all creations of true genius it was a thing of profound simplicity.

The armature is secured by doweling and cementing it into the old arm stump. A mounting ring at the arm interface completes the attachment. Finally, it will be noticed that there is a location pin off-set from the centre of the ring. This allows the armature to be rotated until the exact position is selected to satisfy the sculptor eye, before the pin is driven into the stump to lock the armature in position.

The question now comes up – what material did Camille use to mould the new arm? It is not possible to take a sample for analysis without desecrating the statue. However, the activity that was taking place was also leading to electroplating at a later stage. This being so, the specialist, Danielli, would have been involved.

Danielli must have already been involved in the creation of the original statue since it was here that we discovered the 28% wax content. Therefore, Danielli would have been insisting that the new arm also must use the same material for moulding. It begins to seem that the statue might be an 'experiment' in the use of new technology, primarily the testing of the 'Danielli Method'. If this is so, the emphasis would have been to use only Danielli technology.

The next matter: What's going on in her head?

From the x-ray there would appear to be a lot of damage to repair in the head, presumably caused by the modified-arm ramifications. It might be a reasonable assumption that the [now] upraised hand previously rested on the back of the head (the old classical and hackneyed pose that stretches back centuries). The old arm would not only have to be amputated at the bicep, but the hand would have to be cut away from the head.

That still left questions. Why not just cut away the hand and patch up the hair to match the surrounding area with plaster? If it had been done this way, the X-ray would not have revealed that the head had been disturbed by the arm modification. (There would also have been no clue as to where the original hand had been.)

This situation, rather belatedly, roused us to re-examine the statue. Using a flexible probe into the base cavity, we discovered that, though we could only *see* plaster through the cavity, there were passages that lead deep into the statue interior. *"This statue is hollow!"*

I didn't know how this was done. Terry came to the rescue, having years ago learned how to make non-circular vases. The starting point is the original clay sculpture. From this, a female mould is produced. You then cast the sculpture by repeatedly flooding and draining the mould with a plaster slurry while rotating the mould on two axes so that all surfaces become more or less evenly coated. After several repetitions of this process, a sufficiently thick wall will be built throughout the interior of the mould to achieve a structurally robust product. Later, the plaster cast is removed from the mould. This immediately put one question to rest … we were dealing with a casting, not a moulding. The ragged cavity in the base, it seems, had a purpose. It was, in fact, the entry and drain hole for the plaster slurry.

As this book is a novel we are taking the position that the statue modification is in the charge of Camille Claudel, the patient and highly skilled sculptor and detailer and occasional model for Rodin. She would be very well aware that the statue was hollow.

In dealing with the back of the head, which combined the integrated right hand, she would have sliced off the back third of the skull, removing the piece, hand included. With a keyhole saw, Camille would cut out the hand from the slice of skull. The piece of skull remaining would be like a saucer having a random-shaped hole. Now, addressing the sculpture she needed to build a foundation for the repair work. She filled the head with 'scrunched up' fly-screening, perhaps followed by some wet plaster. She might then press the skull section back in place and strap it all together until the plaster-mesh solidified and, at least temporarily, retained the skull intact.

There would still be the hole where the hand had been, to be dealt with. Now she was into moulding technique rather than casting. This part was quite straightforward and the hair-matching was soon complete.

Camille was still concerned that the back of the head remained too fragile. She came up with an inspired solution. She introduced another armature of wire above the interface of the replaced skull piece. Now she moulded braids tied in a knot at the crown of the head using the wire armature for strength. Structurally the braids now reinforced the repair work, capping off the original saw cut. The *serendipity* of this inspirational solution resulted in an even more beautiful statue.

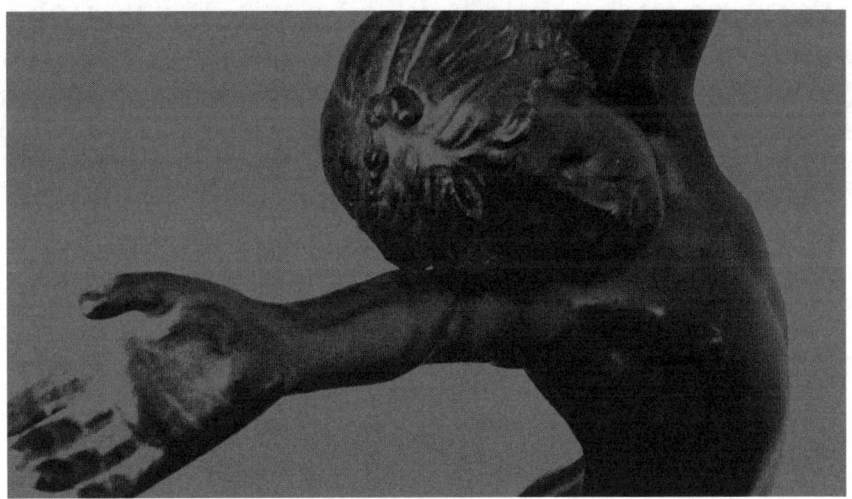

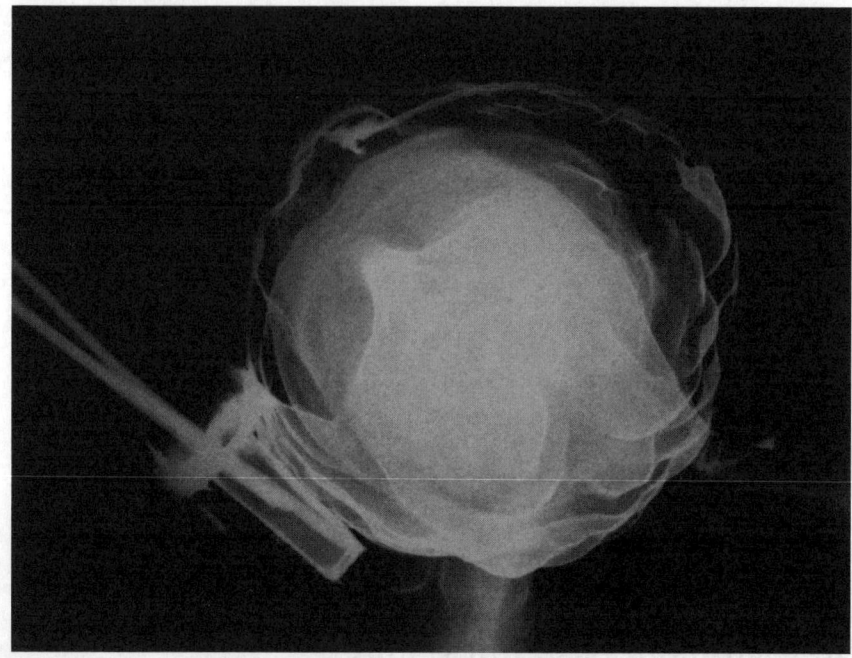

Modified hair-do

We must also remind ourselves again that the plaster has 28% wax content. Therefore, this has to be consistent with the plaster-slurry process. I hark back to Danielli's 'malleable marble' as a product he was planning to sell from his shop at 108 boulevard St. Germain in Paris once the experiments with Rodin were complete. He couldn't sell a boiling water, wax and plaster mix like the one I mixed up and used in my experiment to match the C.C.I. results. It would have to be a homogenized dry plaster of Paris powder and powdered wax mix with instructions to *add boiling water*.

Having extolled the beauty of the armatures in the right arm (the modification) and the new hair-do,

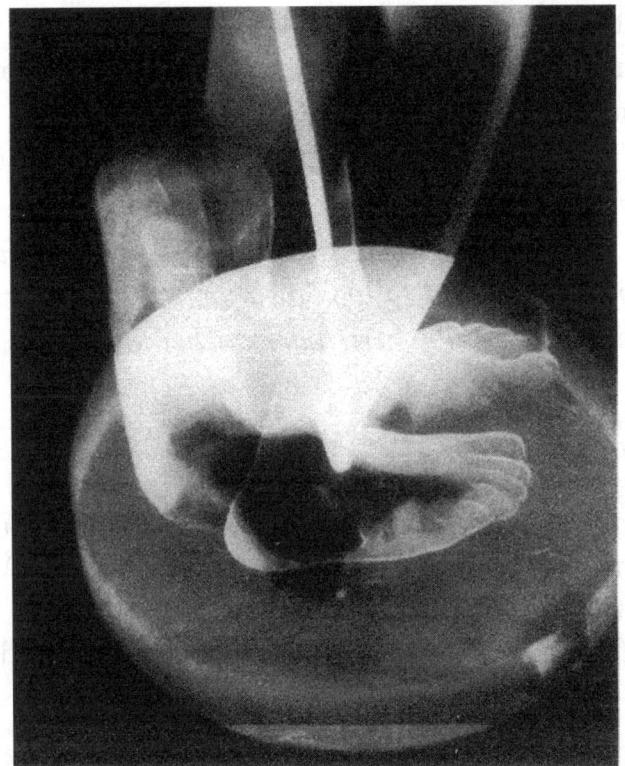

Uninspired foot armature

for the head repair, one is next confronted with the 'foot armature' and reminded of the more common and mundane approach to structural reinforcement. The reason no doubt was that the 3 mm rod that terminated below the hip was probably the best-available material in the scrap-pile. *It would never see the light of day.*

It seems impossible to rationalize that all these armatures came from the same hand. One might guess that the original sculpture and the foot armature were by the 'master'. The modification

93

and the head repairs were the work of the apprentice who had the imagination, the patience and the skill for the task.

"She [Camille] impressed visitors as his most silent and industrious apprentice ... Camille had no time for idle chatter. Wholly absorbed in her work, occasionally she would raise her head to look at a visitor with a quizzical, persistent gaze, then turn back to her work".[2]

Footnotes

1 'From CLAY to BRONZE – A Studio Guide to Figurative Sculpture', by Tuck Langland, Watson-Guptill Publications, New York 1999.
2 'RODIN. A Biography', Frederic Grunfeld, page 214.

13

Turbulent Times

PARIS – September 23 1884

In the Rodin Studio tempers are becoming frayed. It was all about this little statue experiment that was going on.

It seemed that when Danielli turned up and got Rodin interested in the Galvano bronze idea, they started to plot a bit of a joke to spring on the artistic community. The idea was to suddenly produce a statue that had all the attraction of a bronze cast by Rudier, patina and all. But the trick was that it would be so lightweight that one might pick it up and involuntarily toss it in the air in surprise. Rodin even suggested that the plaster cast could be hollow which would make it even lighter still.

Danielli and Rodin got so carried away and they were so secretive that Camille was getting increasingly edgy and downright annoyed for not being in on what ever was going on.

Also Rodin had under-estimated the complications relating to the electroplating. When he was told by Danielli that casting in ordinary plaster would not work and that he would have to use the 'Danielli method' including this powder that he named 'malleable marble', the first sign of irritation started to develop in Rodin. It almost boiled over when Rodin was told that he would have to use boiling water for mixing!

Rodin had hoped that an existing plaster could be dipped in a bath and, hay presto, it would come out bronze-plated. It now looked as if he needed to start with clay and go through the whole bloody Danielli routine from scratch.

It so happened that Antoni Roux was on the prowl again looking to add to his art collection of erotic young women. Rodin had a few on the go in clay, all under the general theme of 'Jeune Fille au bain'. One was a seated nude another standing. One or the other of them might appeal to Roux's taste.

In due course, Rodin and Danielli produced the hollow plaster cast of a standing 'Jeune Fille" using the Danielli plaster mix which Rodin was really beginning to dislike. They decided that before Camille got intolerably angry they had better hold a briefing session. Let her get involved in the Galvano process or something.

But when she saw the plaster cast her fury took off. Glaring at Rodin she screamed "whenever are you going to give up on that hands-behind-the-head pose and **do something different,** for Gods sake?".

Rodin, almost 25 years senior to Camille and almost 20 years to Danielli, decided he had had enough. "Why don't you two get together and finish the damn thing."

He then stalked off in a huff and steered clear of the experimental site. Next day he left for London.

Camille, through the next day made the first effort to get to know Monsieur Danielli for the first time. He was good looking enough, tall and muscular, a shock of black hair and a full beard. He was not much older than she. For all this imposing appearance, he was a quiet and rather shy person. No doubt he was intelligent enough but in matters far removed from her own sphere of interest. He was a chemist and an electrical specialist. She rolled her eyes at the thought.

To break the silence she started. "Monsieur, I have noticed on your visiting card that you have the initial 'J'. Would it be too impertinent of me to ask what 'J' stands for? Danielli responded: "Christen names can sometimes be a problem. Young parents are occasionally foolish and thoughtless, giving their child an inappropriate name, one that leaves he or she embarrassed for life. It can sometimes set the personality on a difficult path. This is my case in a way. I was christened 'Jesus'." With a wan smile he shrugged. "It might explain my shyness, especially with women." Camille had to stifle a giggle and with a straight face replied: "Yes. I can understand that!" He glanced at her eyes, then said softly: "Mademoiselle, why not just call me 'J' and then with your permission I will call you Camille?" She smiled. "If that is your wish, I will certainly do that, Monsieur, but let's treat it as a word 'Jay'. Just between us, from now on it will be Jay and Camille."

The second day after Rodin had left for London, they both felt a feeling of freedom from Rodin's overbearing presence and demands. It was like a holiday.

Jay arrived at the studio shortly after Camille. "How are you Camille?" She shrugged with a slight smile. "I've had a thought," said Jay. "How about taking a day off? I want to go to Montmartre to see the gypsum quarries. Why don't you come along and on the way back we can amble through the Left Bank district, have a meal and see how many famous artists we can spot."

"What a good idea. I would love that." Camille had been a bit depressed ever since her outburst at Rodin. This is just what she needed; to get away from the 'brooding' Rodin studio for a day. On the way there they just chatted about things in general. When they reached the quarries, Jay was in his element.

"You know Camille I am likely to chatter on about gypsum for a bit. Probably nothing you don't know already. Stop me if I get too boring." With that introduction he poked his stick around and scooped up a bit of powder. "Hold out your hand." She did so and he poured a little pile of powder into her palm. Taking her hand in his, he slowly rubbed the powder across her palm with his thumb. "This is the basis for plaster but it needs to be processed. Actually what you are holding is calcium sulphate dihydrate. It only becomes of value to you and all sculptors after it has been roasted at 100 to 180 degrees Centigrade. This causes the gypsum to lose three-quarters of its water-of-crystallization to become usable as calcium-sulphate hemihydrate better known as plaster."

While still looking at the powder in her hand she said "actually I am partly aware of this, though I don't know the chemical terms. Most sculptors either do the roasting themselves as they need it, or buy it from local folk who make a small living by just roasting gypsum. Then, of course we know how to mix this with water to make castings. I do this all the time. It's part of my job even though I didn't know it was calcium-sulphate-hemi...something-or-other," she finished with a laugh.

They looked around and marveled at the size of the quarries. Jay said: "I have been told that the whole of Paris sits on a huge bed of gypsum. If it is deep enough, it could be mined for decades to come without disturbing the city". Apart from shear size, there was not that much to keep them there any longer.

On the way out of the quarries Jay said, almost as if sharing a deep secret: "I wanted to come here and actually see this place. I believe that there is an opportunity here staring us in the face. There is a need for a business group to start a factory for converting this huge store of native gypsum into plaster on a grand scale. This can have many uses apart from sculpture ... from fixing cracks in walls, finishing walls and ceiling, to casting architectural shapes for fancy buildings, maybe even medical uses for repairing fractured bones. This needs to be broadcast through France, Europe, America and even the world. It should be possible for artists and tradesmen to buy it in sacks, labeled and ready to use. It should become known as 'Plaster of Paris' world-wide. What do you think of that wild dream?"

"It's this kind of thinking that makes the world go around, Jay. Do chemistry and electricity absorb all your intellectual interest in life?"

"Actually, no! Before I got into this technical work six years ago, I spent a year in Greece studying their ancient art. I will tell you about that when we find a place for a meal."

They got back into the town at sunset. Jay said "I have been here twice with Rodin. I can't remember the name of the place but I will recognize it when I see it. It seems to be the spot where all the artists gather most nights. When Rodin is along, the famous often gather around to listen to his stories. He strikes quite a presence here".

He soon spotted the place. They found a table, set in the courtyard. Jay ordered a carafe of Bordeaux. For a while it was entertaining to just sit sipping wine and watch those coming and going. Jay said "We're in luck. See in the far corner … that's Paul Gaugin and Vincent Van Gogh deep in conversation". In another area Monet was extolling, somewhat loudly, about his latest trip to London. Jay whispered to Camille. "He thinks the 'pea-souper' fogs have just been arranged for him. He is crazy about the mysterious beauty of a London fog! He paints them all the time." She laughed at this incredibly diminishing summation of such a great artist's work, but let it pass (for now).

'I'm hungry, Jay. Could we get something to eat?" "Of course, Camille. I sometimes talk too much." They settled for an omelette dish with vegetables and a second carafe of wine.

"You know Jay, I am having a really lovely day, I can't thank you enough for inviting me along. By the way, you were going to tell me about your time in Greece."

"Ah yes, that was a happy year. I am sure you know that the outstanding thing about ancient Greece was their passion for personal health and beauty. After absorbing the beauty of so many of the Greek statues, nearly all nudes or revealingly draped, I got to thinking what an experience it must have been to attend the sporting events where all the players were 'perfect specimens', nude and in action. The more perfect they were, the fewer clothes they wore. The gods and goddesses were mostly naked, Venus for example. They were worshiped by the masses that way. But just think of seeing this super-race in action; to see the muscle flow, the suppleness of their movement, their *joie de vivre*." Jay paused ...

"After my first three months in Greece I enrolled in a course on Anatomy at the University of Athens. I thought this was the only possible way of understanding the miracle of the human body ... all creatures for that matter." Looking up apologetically he added: "Sorry, Camille am I boring you?"

"No Jay, You are certainly not. Naturally, as a sculptor I have to have some knowledge of anatomy as do all serious sculptors. But as for formal education, sculptors are all at different levels. In the case of women, it is not even permissible for them to attend anatomy classes. Someday that may change. It was a stroke of good fortune that I got a job with Rodin. Very few women are able to study the human body. Under Rodin I did get an unusual opportunity to be exposed to nudity on a daily basis, to see bodies in action. Did you know that when money is available, Rodin will hire a group of models 'between-assignments' or those 'over the hill' to come to the studio, just to remove their clothes and walk around or exercise, even stand or sit around and chat ? This provides a constant reference to the body-in-motion as Rodin and I work. On some occasions he has had as many as a dozen men and women in at one time. They earn enough to buy their food for a day or so. Working here, as I do, this is always very helpful for absorbing anatomical knowledge by osmosis, so to speak." Jay smiled at the simile that she used. She went on:

"One thing about Rodin is his ability to express movement in his work. When modeling for him I may be just getting ready, taking off my robe, attending to my hair or looking at my nails and he will say 'hold that' and he makes a quick 'clay sketch'... a work of arrested motion. Look at 'L'Age d' arien', for example, or figures in 'Gates of Hell'. They are all caught in action; never posed. Yet here I am in disgrace with Rodin for accusing him of boring poses. I might even have to apologize! But it is good to 'stir the pot' once in a while. I'll have to see what happens'."

"By the way Jay, perhaps you would give me some lessons in anatomy since I can't enrol in a formal class. What do you say?"

Side-stepping that issue, Jay commented on Rodin's anger as he left for London following Camille's outburst about his "boring poses". "Camille, what do you think we should do now?"

She shrugged. "He told us to finish the 'damn thing' ourselves. I interpret this to be a 'carte blanche' go-ahead to finish it any way we choose. Rodin was speaking in the plural you know. We're in this together, Jay! I feel I really have to demonstrate what I mean by making a significant modification of pose to the statue before he gets back, all finished including your 'Galvano Plastique' process, which I would like you to explain to me when the time comes."

"Isn't that a bit risky?" he replied nervously, "I mean you can't start hacking up one of his works without his permission."

"It is mostly about women and his obsession with hands-behind-the-head poses. I am sure you will count that feature at more than 50% if you look back at his studies of women. I have decided to do this modification come-what-may and if he dismisses me....so be-it. I am not afraid of his anger. In my view he'll probably get over it. In any case, I can always support myself with my own sculptures."

Later, Jay escorted Camille to her door, bid her "bon nuit" with a brotherly kiss and was then off to his own lodging.

The Rodin studio on Boulevard d'Italie had shuttered windows. The only illumination was from the skylights. When the doors were locked no one would know if anyone was in here or not. The day would be hot later, especially when the sun started to hit the skylights. Yesterday they had a lovely time and got to know each other much better. Jay and Camille would be working side by side, perhaps for as much as two weeks, entirely alone and undisturbed. Jay was only a few years older than Camille. They were both young and did seem to have things in common after all.

The day had dawned sunny and warm again. Both she and Jay had arrived at the studio quite early intending to tackle the work that was scheduled. Jay was wearing black trousers, sandals, no socks. He had a fresh white shirt with rolled up sleeves and collar open at the neck. He was nicely tanned. She wore some sort of a loose unbleached cotton smock that reached down to mid-calf. It was cinched in by a dark brown sash to emphasize her tiny waist. Otherwise her figure was hidden. These were probably her sculpture work clothes. Her feet were bare. Her auburn hair cascaded wild about her shoulders. After yesterday she felt totally relaxed with Jay for the first time. She was in a good mood; early in the day for her fathomless blue eyes to sparkle so. In point of fact she felt a bit naughty!

"Jay, let me demonstrate the pose modification that I have in mind," she said with a sly smile. Not waiting for a reply she discarded her sash, then turning her back to Jay, she bent her head forward tossing her hair clear of her shoulders. "You will have to unbutton me".

Jay took in a deep breath and his hands started to shake. This was a total surprise for him. He was very shy with women, especially the breathtakingly beautiful ones.

"Come on, Jay," Camille said with a laugh. She seemed perfectly relaxed, acting as if this were a bit of a lark. Her smock had about twenty or so closely spaced buttons between the nape of her neck and the small of her back. As he approached the first button, his fingers touched her neck and she 'jumped' at the coolness of his hands but she said nothing. Each button revealed a little more of her bare skin. It started to appear that she wore nothing under the smock during the unusual warmth of this late summer. Though the studio was cool now and would be until the sun reached the skylight, soon it would be sweltering.

When he was down about twelve buttons he daringly manoeuvred the open sides of the dress just enough to get a first peek at part of her shoulder-blades and the curve of her spine. Her skin was a dusky-creamy colour and had an intoxicating perfume that added to Jay's agitation. Below the last button the smock had an opening of a further ten centimeters or so, with no buttons. As the last button came away, the smock hung loose to reveal almost all of her back. It was beyond his power to refrain from touching her.

More boldly now, he opened his hands and traced his finger-nails lightly and slowly down from shoulders to where the rise to her buttocks began. He had done this only once, when he detected a shift in Camille's mood.

She also seemed to be trembling and her breathing became deeper and more rhythmic. Several minutes seemed to pass before Camille spoke. "I need the buttons at my cuffs undone." Her voice had taken on a husky tone and become almost a whisper as she held her hands forward, forcing Jay to move around to face her.

He took her hands and turned them palm upward. There were three buttons on each cuff, very small in tight little button holes. This was becoming a highly charged operation for both of them. He raised his sights to look into her eyes. Her eyes, as he already knew, were large, blue and incredibly beautiful. But now they had an extra depth that he had not seen before. He noticed also that both he and Camille now seemed to be breathing in unison!

Through all this tension, she could not help smiling at Jay's agitation, in spite of her own. "Remember Jay, this is strictly business for getting the pose correct for the modification." This pulled him back from the brink, as it were, and he struggled with the cuffs for several minutes. Now they too were finally undone.

With her hands at her sides, her cuffs hanging loose, she stood for a few moments with an inscrutable expression, as she faced Jay. Moments later she gave a minute shrug of her shoulders and the smock fell away and pooled around her bare feet. She stood before him, totally nude, proudly sensuous. Jay almost collapsed.

Trying hard to maintain the "business" charade, Camille stepped purposefully onto the model-platform. She said: "Since there is no mirror in here, I will need your help Jay, to keep the statue in sight and guide me into the pre-modification pose. Now don't be shy; you will need to touch me".

By now, Jay was fully aroused and he hoped it didn't show too much. He stepped forward, took hold of her wrists and raised her arms, guiding her hands to grasp the back of her head. As he did this he couldn't help but marvel at the way her body-contours changed in so subtle a manner. In particular, with her arms up, her high pert young breasts flattened noticeably as her rib cage became more defined. She looked very, hmmm, 'sleek'.

"Now the hips," she said; once more in the husky whisper. With his right hand he applied a force to her left hip, pressing it to his left while he used his left hand to apply a balancing force just below her right armpit, to produce the strong thrust of the hips to her right. While doing this he was crouched in front of her. She was just centimeters away. Jay fought to keep control.

He spoke for the first time, stuttering nervously... "N'now while we hold you in this p'po'sition, you need to arch your back as f'far as you can and drop your head si'sidew'ways so that it nestles against your raised upper right arm" … Here! … Er' … l'leme, … let-me help you".

Standing now, he placed his left hand in the small of her back. With his right hand spread as wide as possible, he set his thumb and forefinger on her collar-bone. The palm of his hand then rested centrally on her breastbone. He gradually and gently applied opposing forces to help arch her back.

As she reacted to these forces, Jay felt his left hand signal to his senses, the thrust of her buttocks below and the backward arch of her spine above. His left hand appeared to rest at the pivotal coordinates of her vertebra and pelvis.

There was still one subtly adjustment to make. Jay maintained the pressure of his right thumb against Camille's right collar bone while pivoting his right hand around, removing the pressure on her left collar bone in order to cradled her chin and left cheek in the extended fingers of his hand. He gently applied pressure to turn her face slightly to her right and tilted to more firmly nestle against her raised right upper arm. The forces felt by her spine were now torsional causing her to twist slightly at the waist. (In this final effort, a distinct tremor ran through her body as her breath carried an "ah" to Jay's ear). As all this took place, her breasts now became almost totally flattened, leaving only her nipples marking their position.[4]

Camille's body was so supple and athletic that she managed all this without any visual sign of physical (or mental) distress. She cleared her throat, trying to strengthen her voice, without much success. "Jay, if this looks right to you, remove your hands and I will hold this for a few moments. Walk around me and make sure I looks right from all angles."

Maybe she could "hold this for a few moments" but Jay was surely having trouble. He stood back. He now noticed that her nipples were more evident and had become darker in colour than a few moments ago. The extreme pose also revealed her rib-cage to great advantage, the subtle hollows between, defining each rib. He noticed also the delicate cleft that now developed below the rigidity of her breastbone as the soft tissue and flexibility of her diaphragm yielded slightly under the tensile force within her stretched skin. This cleft extended down almost to her navel. Jay knew enough about anatomy to appreciate that this lovely feature only occurred in the highly tuned female body.

Even a small layer of added fat would obliterate it, especially if her upper abdominal muscles were allowed to deteriorate through lack of exercise. The ancient Greeks knew all about this.

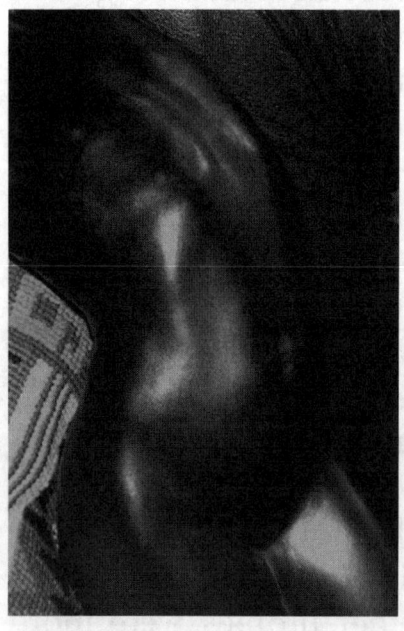

Jay shook his head in disbelief... Camille's body was sheer perfection.

Welcoming the opportunity to hide from Camille's searching eyes for a few moments to recover his composure, he slowly circled around her, taking in every facet of her unbelievable beauty. The most enchanting surprise of all was that a little crease and roll in the flesh had occurred on the concave side of her body (her right side) above her waist, slanting diagonally upwards and toward her back.[3] 'But of course" Jay thought "this results from the turn of her shoulders and the twisting of her waist as I applied the pressure to her chin and left cheek". On her opposite side, her flesh was stretched between rib cage and hip bone, taut like the string of a bow. *[He was later to find that every one of these subtle features had already been captured on the statue by the Maitre, Rodin].* Jay finally faced Camille again. "I will soon be too tired to hold this pose," Camille whispered, showing the first sign of exhaustion. "Let me show you the modification that I plan while I still can ... ready?"

Jay stood back, again in awe. Without changing her body-attitude one iota, and especially keeping the upper right arm perfectly still, she slowly and sensuously raised her lower right arm from the back of her head to stretch upward, rotating her wrist to a palm-upward attitude, her fingers parted and sweeping to the right. Through this move she maintained constant eye-contact with Jay....

Then, satisfied with Jay's reaction, she closed her eyes, took a deep breath then slowly exhaled, slightly parting her now pouted lips.

This was pure magic.[4]

She stepped off the model stand. Jay picked up her sash and smock and handed them to her. She tossed them aside and stepped into his arms. The sun was up now and its heat started to pour through the skylight.

Jay hugged Camille with delight, allowing his hands to run over her body and to experience by tactile senses that he already had memorized through his eyes.

Turning serious, he now gripped Camille by the shoulders. He said: "Camille, we must not get carried away. Put on your clothes and then we must talk". Camille pouted and needed to get herself under control but she did as she was told. She even did up the buttons first and then put the smock over her head and rolled up the sleeves, a technique that took only seconds. This amused Jay as he thought back to the beginning of his adventure with the smock, fighting all those confounded buttons for what seemed like hours.

Jay remained serious. "Camille, I like to be discrete though I cannot help but know of your love affair with Rodin. There is no way that I can allow myself to undermine that relationship."

After a pause he added thoughtfully: "However, we do have one special interest in common. It is our interest in anatomy. You asked me yesterday if I would teach you what I learned as I studied in Athens. I didn't answer you at the time but now I think it would be possible that we could learn from each other. What do you say to that, Camille?"

"Jay, first I find you so gracious and understanding about my situation with Rodin. It is a strange one since he is almost twenty-five years older than me. But he is a man of huge passion and skill as a lover. We have moments of unbelievable happiness. He taught me all I know. I truly love him. You are right though; we must both respect Rodin at all cost." After a few moments of thought, she went on speaking softly: "We cannot hide the fact that the study of anatomy between a man and a woman can become highly erotic. Do you think we could agree on a pact, no matter how aroused we may become, how intense the erotic peaks, during our 'studies', that we shall never, never consummate our relationship while I remain Rodin's lover?"

Jay laughed and said: "You know I believe that the discipline that we must observe in our studies will enhance our erotic experiences and will certainly make them last a great deal longer than otherwise". With this Camille also laughed delightedly. She ran over and embraced Jay as they began to fumble with each others' clothes.

The relentless sun slowly crept over the skylight and poured its heat into the studio. "We will study now ... we can work later when it cools off," she said.[3]

Next day, Camille went to work on the statue. She cut off the right arm at mid-bicep, wrenched the hand from the back of the head and extended it upward on the modified outstretched arm as planned. It was a satisfying "cry of defiance". She was "desperate" for a break from the classical. The future was in Art Nouveau. That's where HER future lay at any rate!

Soon she had finished the armatures, replacing the back of the skull. She repaired the hair, introducing the braids as inspired reinforcement. She was ready to start rebuilding the arm.

Now back to the future. How would she have done this?

In our various musings over the last year or so we had come to refer to the arm as a sub-assembly. I tended to stop doing this when I realized that a 'sub-assembly' implied 'built elsewhere' and plugged in when ready.

I felt sure that she would have had the armature in place, mounted on the stump of the old arm. She would have rotated it to the exact position to her artist-eye and permanently pinned it. Then she would be ready to build the moulding material up on the armature until the final contour was reached to blend exactly with the original statue. This seemed to make sense. Also, in a practical sense, applying the locking pin could only be done BEFORE the moulding took place. It was part of the armature as it shows up on the x-ray.

When I first became seriously involved with the Black Statue research, I imagined the work of the sculptor being more-or-less like moulding a large lump of plasticine. There is, in fact, a little story related in the Grunfeld biography that implies the same thought. It went as follows:

The poet and novelist, Pierre Louys tells a rueful story of an encounter with Rodin in which the youthful bon vivant was quietly outmanoeuvred by a man thirty years his senior. He had met a charming little model in a bar on boulevard St. Germain and she became his mistress. After a short while she disappeared. Some days later, Louys dropped in on his friend Rodin only to find his 'little mistress' posing for Rodin, completely nude. Louys was extremely angry and only calmed down when he saw the figure on which Rodin was working ... "HER IMAGE, ALREADY ALIVE, WAS RISING OUT OF THE CLAY, MORE BEAUTIFUL THAN EVER".[1]

I decided to become more enlightened on sculptural technique. I found *From CLAY to BRONZE* on the internet and bought it through Amazon Books.[2] This straightened me out. In actual practice an unfinished sculpture can have a somewhat gruesome appearance.

"More beautiful than ever, you say!"

As a matter of fact, this photo instantly teaches the technique. As one can see, the figure is built up on the armature one pellet at a time. The pace can be quite leisurely since each pellet as applied is malleable even though those surrounding have hardened. In the case of the arm, the idea is to try to follow the muscle flow.

But as for what material to use, Camille has little choice. She has Monsieur J. Danielli 'breathing down her neck' and pointing out that for the plating process ordinary plaster or clay would erode in the plating bath. She would have to use Jay's 'malleable marble'. Furthermore, she mustn't forget the graphite coating that forms the conductive surface needed for electroplating.

How could she forget it? She didn't even know about it! It's getting more complicated all the time – really aggravating!

Having already upset Rodin and bearing in mind that she was in the middle of changing the pose on one of Rodin's works without his permission, she decided she might need an ally. Better not give Danielli a hard time right now. "Let's get this done!"

The end result was truly unique. *A hollow cast* studio-original with a *molded* right arm modification in *'malleable marble'*, all encased in an 1884-state-of-the-art *proprietary* Galvano Plastique (electroplated) bronze sheath.

Footnotes

1 'RODIN. A Biography', Frederic Grunfeld, page 227.
2 'From CLAY to BRONZE – A Studio Guide to Figurative Sculpture', by Tuck Langland, page 53.
3 A sudden burst of eroticism was unleashed halfway through the chapter when Camille said to Jay "You will have to unbutton me". From that point on the narrative took flight without my conscious influence. The question I have asked myself since is ... "Was there any definable purpose to this?" I have persuaded myself that there was.

I felt there was the need to describe the statue to the readers, for them to appreciate the beauty and difficulty of the pose – one that my own chiropractor indicated "would be close to impossible to hold unless lying down!"

What transpired was the concept of describing the statue in terms of a live model as she was being physically maneuvered, step-by-step, into the extreme pre-modification position. It could also be that I wanted to bring out the beauty of Camille, as represented by the statue. Either way, it seems to make sense; it seemed to be a dynamic approach. The description, using action followed by reaction, was somewhat likened to an engineering analysis. I have since discovered in Grunfeld's "Rodin – a Biogaphy~" that has similar ingredients. The following is paraphrased:

'On one occasion Rodin was to address a group of society ladies but, pleading that he was too exhausted, he had Camille read his speech as he sat alongside. At the end of the speech, Rodin rose "to say a few words" which turned into an *hour-long dissertation comparing architecture to the anatomy of the woman (conmplete with illustrations)"*. This so shocked the puritanical audience that many started to rush their daughters to the exits. Rodin 'soldiered on', seemingly quite obvlivious to the effect he was causing!"

4 The evidence that her breasts, (as observed by Jay) are stretched *flat* by the extreme pose is significant in the controversial debate about "the model's age". Currently – feedback puts this from age 10 to age 17. The research indicates age 19–20, the age of Camille in 1883–4. The low end score is based simply on the fact that the stereotype 'feminine profile' is not visible. All else is dismissed. How does one then explain the mature body-profile of the ballet dancer in full flight during a *'grande jeté'*?

14

The Musée Rodin – Paris

The Musée Rodin stands majestically within spacious grounds on the Rue de Vaurienné quite close to the Eiffel Tower. It is known as Hotel Byron, an old mansion donated by the French Government in 1916 to hold the major collection of Rodin's masterworks.

Out of sight and sound of the 17 tranquil display rooms, there is the mailroom, a large space bustling with activity. There is a huge volume of correspondence daily, delivered by mail as well as a larger volume by fax and still larger yet by email. This comes in at least a dozen major languages.

The operation is set up to sort or sift the content of each delivery according to language and message contained and to redirect for response accordingly. Through this process a low percentage of messages form a 'shortlist' of matters that need to be dealt with by senior personnel, those sensitive to museum policy. This may include matters that could hold potential for forgery, cranky claims of Rodin ownership and anything else that has to be treated strictly within policy guidelines.

Once a month, the shortlist is dealt with by a group of senior staff members from archives, public relations, security and the curatorial departments. My contribution to the shortlist was the package I sent to Paris on February 20, 2002.

By the time it had been passed to a department head and then down for review by staff, it managed to get on the May 9, 2002 agenda for senior review.

PARIS – MAY 9, 2002

The meeting started on time at 10 a.m. After two other cases, the chairperson introduced the package received from Neville Hale by saying that it was internally directed to her and that she had passed it down to her staff for review. She asked Marie to report.

Marie said: "The letter, that accompanied other information, was quite naïve from a provenance point of view. Notwithstanding that the ownership within the Villeneuve and Hale families (linked by marriage) may be provable over 120 years; her opinion was that any link to Rodin was unsupportable. The vague coincidence that Villeneuve and Rodin might have both been students in Paris and for some reason had met and made some financial arrangement or barter was just not credible, let alone provable.

"One reason the package got so far as to reach this committee was partly the indication that M. Hale was prepared to fund a budget in furthering his quest. There was an indication of determination. He was talking to the Canadian Conservation Institute (C.C.I.) about sample analysis, which would be costly.

"But the primary reason, of course, is that the information package attached to his letter had a cover page with the close-up of the statue's face. There seems to be no doubt that the statue he owns, appears to bear a 'Camille face'.

"He believes he has a plaster cast covered with a 'bronze- impregnated black stain' of some sort, but he is not aware of the 'Camille face' or its potential significance. If M. Hale goes further, he has suggested how C.C.I. in Ottawa might interface with our organization in determining any technical clues that might support authentication from samples of material.

"There is also one other point. The statue is completely devoid of markings, either signature or manufacturer's stamp. This fact, at least, seems to minimize the possibility of forgery. Madame, this concludes my response."

The chair thanked Marie and asked others at the meeting for comments. Most thought Marie's report was sufficient for a decision to be made.

The chair then clearly reiterated the rigid policy of Musée Rodin, to NOT confirm OR deny comparisons to Rodin works unless absolute documentation is available as provenance. *The decision is therefore to maintain silence on the matter.* However, it is important that the file be kept open pending any further communications from M. Hale.

Next item.....

The lack of response, as the months passed, caused my quest to be put on the 'back-burner'. In fact it was August 2004 before we started digging deeper and my volunteer research team gradually assembled. It was October 8, 2004, that the '*bombshell*' from the x-rays occurred. It was time to test the waters in Paris for a second go-around.

We decided that first we would 'test the waters' with a simple request to find out whether or not the Museum responded to *any mail*. We had come across a copy of the '*EXPOSITION RODIN*' Catalogue for the year 1900. The cover page had a lithograph by Carrière. It was a black silhouette of a statue in the foreground and Rodin observing it in the background. We asked our previous contact, in a letter dated November 12, 2004, the name of the sculpture and, if possible, the name of the model adding "is it perhaps Camille Claudel?"

The response, prompt and cordial, was received on November 25, 2004. She included full page illustrations of the sculpture known as *'The*

Awakening'. As to the identification of the model she declared that it could not possibly be Camille Claudel because *she had never posed nude for Rodin!* She indicated that the model was probably Anna Abbruzzezi (an Italian with a peasant background) who posed for Rodin in the1880 era.

This 'defense' of Camille was surprising in view of the abundant evidence to the contrary on the internet[1] and in one of several examples from Grunfeld's biography. e.g *p.222: "Camille, however, was quite unabashed about her own sensuality and not unwilling to express it either personally or in clay."*

This work of a strong and mature peasant woman brought to mind Leonardo da Vinci's advice to his students. *"Do not try to exhibit all your knowledge of anatomy by including every muscle in every sculpture. The torso will end up looking like a sack of walnuts!"*

On December 28, 2004, I mailed another letter to Musée Rodin, briefly outlining our recent research that had got underway in August 2004.

From this letter the Musée Rodin would now know that we knew the statue was a 'bronze-over-plaster galvano-plastique'. They would also be aware that tests by C.C.I. revealed the 28% (by weight) wax content in the plaster and, above all, they would have copies of the x-rays and my comment … "that reveal armatures, *suggesting this cannot be a reproduction,* but rather a studio proof or pattern of some kind!" Five other views of the

Black Statue were also included.

Most of our cards were now on the table. This time my letter made the April 2005 meeting.

PARIS – APRIL 15, 2005

The review meeting started at 10 a.m. Four cases preceded the Hale letter, which was then introduced by the chair. She pointed out that the Hale letter had been directed to her and that she had passed this to her staff for review and comment. Again she called on Marie to report.

"In order to prepare a response to the committee, it was first necessary for us to refer to the 'M. Hale' file dated February 20, 2002. We noted at the time that M. Hale indicated a determination in pursuing his quest regarding the origin of his statue. He did, in fact, follow through and obtain an analysis of the plaster material by the Canadian Conservation Institute (C.C.I.). He also knew that the statue was electroplated by the so-called 'Galvano-Plastique' method.

"More importantly, M. Hale obtained access to an x-ray machine capable of photographing the entire statue within three shots." Prints of the x-rays taken were enclosed.

The mention of an X-ray immediately caught the full attention of the committee. Marie pressed a button on the lectern and the blinds above the window silently lowered. A second button lowered a projection screen and a third button powered the projector.

A projection of the right-arm X-ray, many times life-size, stretched across the whole screen where it was scrutinized by every member for several moments while silence reigned. After a long pause, Marie continued.

"There is nothing in the x-rays that specifically links his statue to Rodin or, indeed, to any other artist. However, the interpretation of the armature in the statue's right arm leaves little doubt that the right arm is a skillful modification of pose to an earlier statue. There is no indication by M. Hale that he is aware there may be a connection between the face of the statue and that of Camille.

"I believe that brings the status up-to-date. Madame, this completes my report."

The chair thanked Marie and called for discussion.

A member pointed out that whereas M. Hale had made considerable progress technically, *there was no change in status from the viewpoint of provenance* and he therefore moved that the Musée Rodin remain silent on the subject.

Another member emphasized that the x-rays proved that a *connection to "some studio" must have existed in order to produce such an obviously skilled pose modification.* There could be a concern or, at least, a change in status, if M. Hale were to start comparing the face of his statue to that of Camille. This was especially so if some credible scientific method of comparison were introduced. This, if judged valid, together with the "some studio involvement" scenario, would provide the essence of total proof linking the Black Statue to the Rodin studio.

A third member emphasized that the lack of signature or manufacturing mark did have a precedent. Rodin was known to occasionally give gifts of plasters to friends, that were unmarked.

The chair ruled that the silence be maintained on the strength that a document link between Rodin and Villeneuve remained a virtual impossibility. According to museum protocol and policy, no authentication would likely be issued even if the statue was proven authentic on technical grounds alone. *Provenance was an essential part of authentication.*

"We shall keep the file open should further developments materialize."

"Thank you. If there are no further questions, this meeting is adjourned."

PARIS – JANUARY 12, 2006

The monthly review meeting started at 10 a.m. The meeting was brought to order and a number of routine items were attended to. There were two other cases relating to incoming mail of policy sensitive issues. Then the Hale file was up for discussion. The chair asked Marie to make her report.

Marie reminded the committee that the last discussion on the 'Black Statue' affair had been on April 15, 2005 where it was decided to continue to maintain a silence based on "policy". She now had to report that a letter dated October 20, 2005 had been received. This package contained a copy of a book written by M. Hale entitled "*Hall of Mirrors – The Black Statue Mystery*". This contained the factual progress of research up to date within the setting of a 'non-fiction novel'. The letter, in particular asked if it were possible that a Musée staff member might be tasked to read the book and report to their department head on their findings.

"The significant new item revealed in the book was the description of a mathematical process for comparing the face of the Black Statue and the famous photo portrait of Camille at age 19, dated 1883. The test included five other faces, all of which were chosen for a degree of visual likeness to that of Camille. In each case, measurement ratios (e.g. eye spacing divided by eye-to-mouth measurements etc.). The ratios computed for each subject were compared with the same ratios for the statue. Results were presented in the form of 'mismatch %' where a perfect score would be 0.00%.

"This scheme was generated in response to Rodin's reported tendency to utilize "a Camille face" on a number of appropriate statues whether-or-not she was the model in question.[2] By this process, the mismatch for Camille was 3%. The other 'test faces' ranged from 17% to 28%.

"It was M. Hale's conclusion that the combination of the x-ray findings revealed at the previous meeting, when supported by a persuasive face-match, was powerful evidence that the Black Statue was *a studio original* (x-ray evidence) and that *the studio had to be the Rodin studio* (face-match evidence).

"It has to be reported also that the book was passed down to a staff member for review and reporting. This is underway but no report has yet been tabled. During the process, one hand-written communication from the Musée Rodin went to M. Hale, suggesting that the Black Statue and some works by Jean Leon Gerome had strong similarities. If this were intended to move M. Hale's focus from Rodin to other artists, it was not entirely successful. M. Hale responded to the handwritten note on December 11, 2005. He pointed out that he saw the similarity of an extreme pose, but on research of Gerome there was no indication that he had ever worked in Galvano Plastique. This led to a newly claimed proof, based on provenance issues, as follows:

"It was known that M. Hale's father Percy Edward Hale, was born in Clerkenwell, London, on August 15, 1887. His mother, Isabella Villeneuve, was married to Edward Hale by 1886. According to family lore, Isabella received the Black Statue from her father, as a wedding present. This indicated that the statue was accepted in 'payment of a debt', probably no later than 1885.

"Continuing with this argument, it is known that J. Danielli, the inventor for electroplating plaster and other non-conductive materials, first made contact with Rodin in 1881 to propose a *proprietary partnership* in developing the 'Danielli method' technology (later renamed Galvano Plastique). Research indicated that between 1881 and 1885 this new technology was held secret from artists beyond the Rodin studio. As such, the receipt of the statue by Villeneuve *must have come from Rodin or his agent during the period that the Galvano Plastique remained proprietary to the Rodin studio.*

"Madame chair, this completes my report."

"Unless there are any questions we will schedule another review after we receive a report on the content of M. Hale's book." She was about to close the meeting when one member spoke up.

"Madame chair, I feel disturbed that M. Hale has produced so much evidence over four years against....

and I say this with respect.... discouraging tactics by the Musée. There are now three sources of carefully prepared evidence by M. Hale that make it almost impossible for this committee to continue ignoring the obvious, simply by relying on a narrow reading of Musée policy. I believe it is time to start dialogue."

A second member countered: "Part of the problem may be that the statue appears to be an experimental piece, intended only to prove the Galvano Plastique technology that was abandoned by Rodin following the plating of the St. Jean plaster. It is not a 'Rodin', it is a 'Rodin studio product' involving, no doubt, Monsieur Danielli and Mille Camille Claudel to a great extent. The statue winds up in a most uncharacteristic pose and a braided hairstyle, never before or after, appearing in his work. It is an anomaly. I feel sure that it was never intended for public display. Its final fate was to use it as currency to a non-collector for quiet disposal outside the country. It was Rodin's intention that it 'vanish into history'."

One other member, clearly annoyed by the negativism of the last speaker, spoke up: "For an artist such as Rodin, just the sweepings from his studio floor would be a collectors' item, cherished by many a collector today. Is it the viewpoint of this committee that involvement by Camille Claudel.... *the discovery of a Claudel/Rodin original....* is NOT of value to the Musée? Rodin himself honoured Camille with a room dedicated to her work. Is it NOT important to the Musée Rodin that the discovery of *a joint-work* by these two great artists,... at the peak of their love affair ... has now been discovered? *There is a gem out there.* We have a duty to recognize that and act accordingly."

On this divisive note the chair herself, clearly annoyed, decided to close the meeting with these words: "I have seen the book. It has no more than 100 pages, no more than a two-hour read. I will follow up and arrange for a report to be available for the next scheduled meeting. This meeting is adjourned." The committee walked out in silence pondering the final exchange.

Footnotes

1 http://www.cs.wusl.edu/~loui/camille.html – page 3.
2 'RODIN. *A Biography'*, by Frederic Grunfeld, pages 242–243.
3 The name '*HALL OF MIRRORS. The Black Statue Mystery'* was later changed to '*THE RODIN QUEST. The Black Statue Enigma'* for an expanded version of the same story. Publication is anticipated in the U.K. in 2006.

15

The Antoni Roux Equation

We were to make one further communication with Musée Rodin. This concerned one of Rodin's wealthy clients, a collector named Antoni Roux. He liked to buy exclusivity. One of these negotiations caught my eye as reported on page 206 of Grunfeld's 'RODIN. A Biography'. This was regarding a sculpture described as "a small figure entitled *Jeune Fille au bain*".

Rodin made the sale and to satisfy Roux, included a written agreement that he [Rodin] would refrain from making any reproductions.

On May 25, 2005 we sent an email to the Musée Rodin requesting information and hopefully an illustration of this work. Our reason was that the name '*Jeune Fille au bain*' perfectly fitted the Black Statue. An immediate reply confirmed the arrival of the email at the museum and assurance that within a short while the information would be sent to us.

A reply by airmail arrived about June 17, 2005 with the information requested. Although it was not the same pose as my statue, there was some interesting information included in two attached articles.[1, 2] The following is an edited down version of the articles received. The first article by Albert E. Elsen of the Cantor collection in California, There was a photo of the actual *'Jeune Fille au bain'* that Rodin originally sold to Roux, which now resides in the California Cantor collection.

The statue was dated 1888 which was about the date of the sale, but the true date of sculpture was qualified as being actually three or so years earlier. *"The work has the look and finish of the early 1880s and George Grappe conceded it was made before 1888"*.[1] It did, indeed, seem to have similarities to my Black Statue in general appearance. (The date around 1884–5 matches other research conclusions regarding first ownership of the Black Statue by Villeneuve.)

From the accompanying letter that we received It appears that the statue *Jeune Fille au bain* was also known as *'Bather Zoubaloff'* from the name of the man who bought a plaster of this sculpture at the sale of the Roux collection.

The second article was authored by Mme. Antoinette Romaine of the Musée Rodin.[2] This article addressed *'Bather, Bather Zoubaloff'* dated before 1888. The dimensions given were smaller

Jeune Fille au bain.

The Black Statue

than my statue, but part of the text went on as follows:

"Roux wanted unique studies, so he asked Rodin to [always] give him the bronzes **and** the plaster casts. This was true of Bather of which he owned both the plaster cast (Jacques Zoubaloff collection, then the Rodin Museum) and the bronze (not found). The catalogue of his scattered collection in Paris mentioned that they were accompanied by a receipt from September 24 1888 in which Rodin stated that henceforth the piece would not be reproduced but that TWO OR THREE STUDIES IN PLASTER HAD PREVIOUSLY BEEN GIVEN TO FRIENDS. **There were, no doubt, many of these studies and it seems they were not only plaster casts** (of which we actually know of several like the ones in Buenos Aires) but also bronzes and **castings with no mark** which had belonged to collector-friends of Rodin and had been seen on the market."

This rather subtle and complicated dissertation is merely included to emphasize the fact that *plaster casts with no mark, were created by Rodin and were known to exist, there was a precedent*. It might have been the custom for Rodin *not* to sign works that he presented as gifts or *not* to sign works that were involved with exclusivity agreements, to try and encourage new owners to retain rather than sell them. Whether this worked or not is all part of *hall of mirrors* within which Rodin seemed to operate.

My interest is that within this jumble there may be an indication that I hold a spin-off from the 'Rodin-Roux circus'.

Before leaving the discussion *vis a vis* Antoni Roux, there is a footnote on page 187 of the Grunfeld biography of Rodin which may answer the question "why would a sculptor modify a statue?". One answer is obvious ... to satisfy a client. A second answer might be ... to create a new work at less cost and effort!

I quote verbatim from Grunfeld biography – (French inserts omitted).

"In 1885, Rodin used the same 'falling man' module to create still another variant, this time at the request of Antony Roux, who had asked him for a man with a snake instead of a man with a woman. It was a commission that he accepted with misgivings, since the idea had not originated with him. "It is agreed" he wrote to Roux, "but my etude remains as it is and I shall make no modifications for myself. It is for you that I am making the changes, and it is in order to enter into the subject 'Man Struggling with a Serpent' that I change the arms". The figure as a whole appears in at least one other assemblage, and the torso was enlarged to lead a separate existence as 'marsyas', or as Torso Louis XIV. See John Tancock's *The Sculptures of Auguste Rodin*. Pp 163–167'."

Footnotes

1 *'RODIN'S ART'* by Albert E. Elsen and Rosylin Frankel Jamison. The Iris and Gerald B. Cantor Centre for Visual Arts at the Stanford University. This is stamped with Seal 'Musée Rodin Bibliotheque' # Inv 20722.
2 Rodin en Buenos Aires. Antoinette Le Normond. Romaine. This is stamped with Seal 'Musée Rodin Bibliotheqe' # Inv 20328.

16

The Coded Signature

It is her face that is the most controversial. Those familiar with Rodin's work declare, without fail, "the face is not a Rodin!" Some point out that there is no anguish, no pain, no grief. It is far too tranquil a face to be a Rodin. I thought as much the same when I visited the Rodin Exhibition at the ROM in 2001. As I first walked around I said to myself "I don't have a Rodin".

But this was before we identified the Rodin studio *team* and we became aware of Camille's influence. *"We know Camille's hand whenever we see demure sweet innocence (as opposed to melodrama lacking emotional candor)"*.[1]

Camille's presence created the 'sweet period' through the 1880s. Most exhibited works at the 2001 exhibition emphasized later works (after 1894), and a few earlier works (before 1882). These periods might be called 'unbiased Rodin's'; focused on the idolization of physical form, religious and political themes, that is to say, works un-influenced by Camille.

At that time, we had not discovered the quote from the Grunfeld biography: "He [Rodin in later life] had never forgotten his *"sagacious and clairvoyant collaborator, his élevée and her face had continued to appear in his later statues"*.[2]

Here at last is the missing clue. This discovery[2] is to say that her face appeared on appropriate works *during and after* their collaboration and affair, *whether or not she served as a model as well as a sculptor.*

A resemblance between Camille and the Black Statue therefore, must be considered as a form of signature on an unsigned work!

This thought will be pursued, and encouraged, by a parallel discovery from a research team member. After reading background literature behind Dan Brown's *'Da Vinci Code'*, he reported: "One of the more scholarly books was discussing the speculation that the Mona Lisa is a self-portrait of Leonardo dressed (or reincarnated) as a woman. They [researchers] took measurements of features of the Mona Lisa face, and features of the face in a self-portrait of Leonardo, as a bearded old man, *and they calculated 'coincidences'."*

In the next chapter we will take a similar approach using mathematics to compare *face ratios* of the Black Statue to the Camille photo portrait and to other test faces.

Footnotes

1 www.cs.wustl.edu/~loui/camille page 3 of 7 (Camille's influence).
2 *'RODIN. A Biography'*, Frederic Grunfeld, pages 242–3 (Camille's face transplanted on other works).

17

Unlocking The Final Secret
Not Just a Pretty Face

In October 2001 I took the opportunity to have an appraiser look at the Black Statue for the first time. It was a charity event at the village of Craigleith on Georgian Bay. They staged an 'Antiques Traveling Road Show' format. My wife and I waited in line for hours as, one by one, those ahead of us shuffled forward to display their treasures to one of two appraisers on duty.

Our spirits were kept up by the conviction that we had something to display that was in a class of its own. "It could cause a riot when it's unveiled."

When we finally got our turn, the appraiser picked my statue up, turned it this way and that, and said "it has no signature!" He called to his partner, "this has no signature", to which the partner replied "Let it go. Impossible to put a value". End of discussion. No riot.

But then the appraiser kept looking at my statue for what seemed like an eternity. Then he sighed sadly and said, almost to himself: "Whoever would create a statue this beautiful and not sign it?" With this thought we left.

It was worth our while to spend half a day of discomfort, just to hear that question *asked by an expert*. I started to think of scenarios that might provide an answer.

1. If the statue were a forgery, the forger would include the name of a well-known artist to establish illicit value.
2. If the statue was a reproduction one would expect some identification of the manufacturer, or a stamp of some kind.
3. What if it was the work of a talented student or apprentice to an established artist, he/she would be told to sign it to avoid confusion with the artist's own work. They would be proud to do so.
4. But what if the artist was self-critical and this was his own work? He might judge the Black Statue as insignificant, and stick it up on the shelf. Or it might have been a pattern (a foundry plaster) that had been used for creating a bronze. Maybe it was put aside to be used as 'currency' to pay off a debt once it had achieved its initial purpose. Or was it an experimental piece?

In the summer of 2004, a similar show was put on in Collingwood, somewhat better organized in that one had a time-slot during the day rather than stand in line. By this time I had done a lot of reading about Rodin. I had also established a link with the Canadian Conservation Institute in Ottawa for them to examine a sample of the modeling material that I was able to reach through a cavity in the statue's base. There was more to talk about.

On this occasion, the show was running late, everyone was tired. The reception was almost hostile, referring to the statue as "sentimental Victorian reproduction", a "poor man's bronze". "Really you shouldn't waste any more time on it!" My fifteen-minute booking was squeezed down to five minutes. It was virtually a monologue.

But all this preceded the discovery that *Rodin used Camille's face on works for which she did not necessarily model*. On being confronted by a side-by-side photo presentation of the faces of the Black Statue and Camille, a slim majority of observers tended to admit, without that much conviction, to a "reasonable likeness". We needed something more precise than this.

I entered the 'Face Morphology' business, a mathematical process that can have many levels of sophistication, especially in this present age of sophisticated crime and terrorism. Security has become big business and a new science. Companies with this expertise compete for hugely expensive government contracts.

But one can stand back and reason that, *for us*, we just need the answer to the simple question: "How closely does Camille's photo portrait match the face of the statue?" We don't need 'rocket science' but we do need a bit of 'mathematics 101'. We need to measure and compare a number of characteristic face-ratios (e.g. eye spacing/mouth width; chin to eyeline/eyeline to hairline)

For those with a 'bent' for mathematics this is pretty obvious stuff. For those otherwise inclined, please accept that I, the author, *am* mathematically inclined. I know what I'm doing. If all the 77 measurements for this scoring process, as taken by me, are tolerably accurate, then this accuracy will be reflected in the accuracy of the computer-calculated score. Believe me folks, this is NOT 'rocket science', nor does it need to be.

When I was explaining to my grandson what I was trying to do, he commented: "All faces may be the same, grandpa. You need to also test other faces!" I did and they all were *decisively outscored* by the statue/Camille match.

For the other faces, we selected three photos of Audrey Hepburn, two prior to her spectacular fame and under totally different photographic circumstances to each other, one candid and the other a highly refined advertisement The third Audrey photo was at age 63 as she worked heroically for the starving children in Africa, shortly before her own untimely death.

The fourth contender was a portrait that survived fifty years, from the days about 1954–5 when I took a sabbatical from engineering and opened a photographic studio in Niagara-on-the-Lake. It was of a girl, aged about sixteen, that I (much later) named *'Eye Contact'*. No record of her name exists. Finally we included the *'Mona Lisa'*, more of an attention-grabber than a contender (particularly as she is smiling).

Therefore, each of these contenders underwent the identical measurement analysis to that of Camille, to provide a mathematically comparative score. On the next page, we assemble the results.

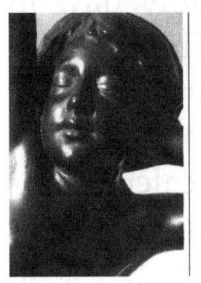 

CHARACTERISTICS
OF THE FACE

Comparison between the face of Camille and the face of the Black Statue

MISMATCH 3.03%

Where a perfect score = 0.00%

Audrey Hepburn 1951 – A candid photo during an off-stage coaching for the Broadway production, *'Gigi'*.

MISMATCH RELATIVE TO STATUE **27.94%**

Audrey Hepburn 1992 at age 63, working in Africa for the starving children and aids related tragedies, shortly before she, herself, died.

MISMATCH RELATIVE TO STATUE **18.40%**

Audrey Hepburn – 1951 at age 22 from an advertisement for a skin lotion.

MISMATCH RELATIVE TO STATUE **28.81%**

A studio photo by the author in 1954, entitled *'Eye Contact'*. (There is no record of the name of the model.)

MISMATCH RELATIVE TO STATUE **17.92%**

'MONA LISA' – Leonardo da Vinci , 1502

MISMATCH RELATIVE TO STATUE **23.05%**

Rodin was quoted as saying that the only flaw in Camille's beauty was her weak chin. The primary reason for selecting the Audrey Hepburn and '*Eye Contact*' photos was a weakness of chin in all cases. Despite this mutual weakness, the calculations decisively separated the 'Camille mismatch' at 3.03% from all others that ranged from 17.9% to 28.81%.

When everyone, including myself, were saying the face of the Black Statue is NOT A RODIN, could it be that Camille's face is 'THE CODED SIGNATURE' proving the statue IS A RODIN?

18

"The Truth Will Out"

So there it is! We have arrived, at last, with two key discoveries, *both of which must be present to solve the mystery.*

The x-ray revealed in chapter 12 displays extraordinary skill in performing a modification to an earlier statue. This proves the involvement of an unidentified studio operation. It also proves that the Black Statue cannot be a reproduction.

The match between the face of the Black Statue and the photo-portrait of Camille Claudel – Chapter 17 – proves a Rodin involvement. On its own one could argue that the Black Statue could still be a reproduction. But obviously, the presence of the x-ray proves otherwise.

There is also other persuasive evidence. For example, it is significant that the pose-modification we see in the x-rays, (Chapter 12), *had to precede* the electroplating process. This required the presence of Danielli. *Only he possessed 'the magic' of how to apply bronze coating to plaster when he first knocked on Rodin's door in 1881.*

During the lengthy period that Danielli and Rodin experimented together, *the electroplating technology – the Galvano Plastique – remained proprietary to the Rodin studio. This eliminated other players!*

Danielli had to be present earlier also, in the creation of the original statue. A sample of the casting material from the original statue, that was tested by CCI in Ottawa in 2004, (Chapter 10), was shown to contain 28% paraffin wax, *indicating Danielli's specification for waterproofing the plaster in readiness for plating.*

Among all the technical clues and arguments that come to mind it is, nevertheless, Camille's face, the face that all declared could not be a Rodin, that comes hauntingly into focus as the key to the truth we have been seeking.

There is now no doubt that the Black Statue had it's origin in the Rodin Studio. *The only mystery that remains: how was it that Theodore Villeneuve wound up as the owner?*

Read on.

19

Rodin Goes to London

The question of London first came up while Rodin was working on the bust of Legros. They had been reminiscing about their time in the National Guard in 1870 when Paris was under siege. After the end of the siege in January 1871 they had independently decided to leave Paris. The war had left Paris relatively unscathed structurally, but in ruins economically. There was no work to be had for artists; for Rodin, sculpture and drawing and for Legros, etching and painting.

Rodin went north to Brussels where he worked as an ornamentalist by day while he pursued his own work by night. Legros chose London. Rodin at the time was virtually unknown to the art world at large, while Legros had already a degree of fame as an etcher. Thus Legros fairly quickly landed a position on the faculty of the Slade School of Art in London, as Professor of Drawing.

The Slade School was rapidly building an impressive reputation by the late 1870s. Those with positions there started to move up in society. Legros developed many influential connections and friends.

In the meantime, in 1878 Rodin produced one of his most famous works, '*Age d'airain*'. As related in Chapter 1, this work was the cause for an attack on Rodin's reputation by the establishment. There was no foundation to the scandal that had hurt Rodin very deeply. He hated the publicity, he didn't seek fame, yet now his work was being noticed, and would continue to be propelled by his genius long after the malicious scandal had burned itself out.

There was no doubt about it, by 1880 and in Paris, Rodin was 'the talk of the town'.

And so it was in 1881, as Rodin worked on the bust of Legros it seemed opportune for Legros to start urging Rodin to broaden his horizons and accept an invitation to be his guest in London.

Legros had 'gone overboard' for London. He had acquired an English wife, English children and British nationality. They were raising the family in a rambling house at 37 Brook Green, Hammersmith, just west of the capital. Rodin was later to find out that they only spoke French in the Legros home. This suited Rodin very well and it seemed that Legros had made little effort to learn English himself. When he was teaching at the Slade he spoke only French, which a fair number of students could follow. When he needed to speak to individual students who didn't understand French, Legros would simply appoint one of the students who did, to act as an interpreter.

As for travel it couldn't be simpler now there was the 'boat-train'. You board the train in Paris. When you reach Boulogne the ferry takes you across the channel to Folkestone where the train is waiting to take you on to London. It only takes 10 hours during which you can read, write, sketch or sleep and dream, a wonderful opportunity to spawn new ideas.

And so it was that Rodin finally accepted the invitation from Legros and he made his first of many regular visits to London in 1882.

Legros was a superb host. He walked Rodin through all the museums. The British Museum, which was just around the corner from the Slade, was a favourite for many reasons, but especially the display of the Greek 'Elgin Marbles'. Rodin was to say the 'Three Fates' from the pediment of the Parthenon were "the most beautiful thing Greece ever produced". Legros, too, was a passionate admirer of the Elgin Marbles. Once when a friend suggested that the sculptures should be returned to the Greeks, he burst out "Not on your life! I'd take a gun and man the barricades".[1]

One wet day, Legros hired a 'Hansom Cab' for the day's tour. The Hansom Cab was a two-wheel conveyance propelled by a single horse.[2]

A mix of Hansom cabs and trade vehicles on a London Street –
1882.[3]

To tour Victorian London in all its beauty from this vantage point must have been an unbelievable experience for Rodin as the framed panorama constantly changed before his eyes. He had even extolled about the beauty of the green and yellow fogs and the ruddy colour of the buildings in the late afternoon haze as the sun was setting. A rainy day would have also been just another perfect environmental experience. He now understood the fascination that had captivated his friend Monet, whose paintings of such scenes were already famous.

By later visits, Legros had mobilized his circle of acquaintances on Rodin's behalf. He introduced the sculptor to the influential art collector Constantine Ionides and to the president of the Royal Academy Sir Frederick Leighton; to Robert Browning and to W. E. Henley, author of the poem Invictus: *"Under the bludgeoning of chance, my head is bloody but unbowed"* … *"I am the master of my fate, I am the captain of my soul"* and other rousing lines!). Henley was one of the leading magazine writers of London.[1]

Henley, in particular, became Rodin's chief 'apostle' in the promotion of his work in London until, he himself died in 1906. Henley was buried in the crypt of St. Paul's Cathedral. The tomb included a special recess to inset his bronze bust created by Rodin, where it can be seen to the present day.

Rodin traveled to London more and more frequently as the years went by. The excuse was to attend functions and exhibitions. *His real reason was that he now loved London with a passion.*

Footnotes

1 'RODIN. A Biography', by Frederic Grunfeld, pages 138–140.
2 The cabin of the "Hansom" cab was enclosed on three sides and a roof but open at the front. The driver or 'cabby' sat behind, and partly above, the enclosed cab from where he held the reins to guide the horse. If the passengers wanted to communicate with the cabby there was a small trap-door in the roof. Tap on that with ones umbrella and the door would open and the cabby's face would peer down ready to take instructions.
3 H.R.H. The Prince of Wales *'A VISION of BRITAIN – A Personal View of Architecture'*.

20

The Meetings

Through the association with W. E. Henley, Rodin would visit London frequently for the next 30 years. However, it was only in the first few years that Rodin felt inspired to bring back to Paris, gifts for both Rose and Camille, making sure that they never met to compare their gifts. As the London trips became more frequent and longer in duration, the present-giving tailed off in both his mind and in the expectation of his women. The travel had become just routine.

It was on one of his early trips to London in late 1884, when travel was still exciting, that a special gift for Camille started to form in his mind. Just a month or so earlier he had a devastating row with Camille. It was when he discovered that she had, without his permission, modified the pose on one of his works. He was still depressed that they may never recapture the love and respect they once had for each other.

In spite of the travesty of her act he had to admit that her sudden attack on him, a criticism that the poses he used were boring and hackneyed, might have held some truth. *"When will you do something new, for God's sake,"* she had screamed. He had walked out in a huff after telling her to *"finish the damn thing yourself"*. She did just that. With her young mind and enthusiasm she decided *to demonstrate* what she meant.

Rodin realized now that what also might be in her favour was the fact that the work in question (one in the series of the theme, *'Jeune Fille au bain'*) had been selected by him for experiments in new technology, specifically the Galvano Plastique (electroplating over plaster – the 'Danielli Method'). Therefore this was not slated to be a work that would ever be displayed in public, and eventually might even be scrapped or used as currency with a non-collector. He had to face it – his pride was the problem!

He did not relish the idea of humbly admitting that she was right and his work was boring. He thought instead that a special and spectacular gift, perhaps a gift for her 21st birthday coming up on December 8 next year, would serve the purpose better than words. This would also leave plenty of time to decide what to do and how to bring it about.

As the train was chugging up from Folkestone towards London, he pulled out his sketchbook and started doodling. After a while he centered on a wide bangle to be worn on the upper arm, maybe gold or perhaps silver. But how to make it decorative? One could roll the edges and, maybe beat some texture into the surface.

Then he hit on the concept. He would produce a *miniature 'Jeune Fille au bain'* reclining on the wide band of silver, her back arched to follow the sweeping curve. Her right arm would be raised, her hand resting on the rolled edge of the silver band. He hoped that by introducing the *raised* right arm, Camille would interpret this to be a forgiveness of her "travesty", an unspoken *"you were right about the pose"*. The figure would be cast in solid gold. The silver she lay upon would simulate water in contrast to the gold.

This miniature figure (about 7 cm tall) would be the only reclining version of the *'Jeune Fille'* series and would not violate any upcoming exclusive sale to Antoni Roux. (Roux eventually chose the seated *'Jeune Fille'*).

To pull off this idea and to keep it a secret, Rodin decided he would need to work with a goldsmith in London. Rodin had planned to be in England for the next few weeks. *"There will be time to find the right goldsmith to sound out the idea, to get agreement in principle on a plan."*

Rodin would, of course, produce the miniature

sculpture in plaster. He might also make the female mould. These he could best do in Paris. The casting in gold would be done in London and the silver work would be done in London also. Method of payment for the goldsmith's work and materials would need to be discussed at their first meeting.

Looking for a goldsmith became fairly straight forward. Once settled back in London, he was advised by Legros to go to the local library and ask to see a copy of *'The Business Directory of London'*. This he did and he learned that the gold and silver trades were centered in the Clerkenwell district of Central London. Under the classification 'Gold', all the jewelers of London were listed. It was easy therefore to hunt for those that had a Clerkenwell address.

It wasn't long before one name 'jumped out' from the others. It was a French name 'Villeneuve'. This jogged something in Rodin's memory. The name was familiar, but why? Then he remembered that Camille spent her childhood in Villeneuve-sur Fère. In fact Rose and he had been invited to lunch by Camille's family shortly after Camille was hired as an assistant at the studio. Villeneuve-sur-Fère was east of Paris on the road to Reims. More important was the fact that Rodin would be able to communicate so much better if he and the goldsmith spoke the same language.

Checking again, the directory stated *Villeneuve, Theodore, 28 Northampton Square, Clerkenwell*. There were four other jewelers located at the same little square and several more dotted around and further afield. This looked like a focal point of the industry. A map of London showed him how to reach that address from the British Museum, a spot he already knew quite well. It was less than two miles east. He listed the names of the streets he needed to follow.

THE FIRST MEETING – LONDON – sunny and cool.
DECEMBER 7 1884. 11 a.m.

28 Northampton Square, Clerkenwell
(as it stands today, January. 2006)
The site of the Villeneuve jewelry and goldsmith
business in the 1870s and 1880s[1]

Behind this door the historic barter was set — 1884[2]

The meeting place for Rodin and Villeneuve. The exchange of the Black Statue for jewelry took place here in 1885.

Rodin stood outside No. 28 for a moment or two. The sign was simple, 'VILLENEUVE AND SONS – GOLD'. The building was built in that ruddy coloured brick, a patina resulting from London's notoriously harsh atmosphere. This was the colour that Monet raved about and immortalized on canvas. The trim was white and there were black wrought-iron railings leading up to the front door and down to a basement area. There were upper floors that may have been living quarters. It was a 'terrace house' [town house], one of several in a row.

When Rodin entered the shop, a grey-haired man of about 60 or so was talking to another customer. A younger man was at the buffing machine polishing a gold item. Rodin had time to wander around looking at examples of Villeneuve's work. He was clearly a highly skilled goldsmith. When the other visitor turned and left, Villeneuve asked softly "may I help you?".

Rodin explained that he was from Paris and that he was looking for a goldsmith to collaborate with him on a special piece of jewelry. Villeneuve said in French "please come in, we can sit at my desk".

They got comfortable and chatted about generalities for a few moments. Rodin then drew out his sketchpad at a blank page. As he started to explain the piece he had in mind, he drew with sure sweeping lines, the bangle. "I am thinking that this should be of silver and the upper surface should be textured to simulate water. My own contribution to the work will be to produce a miniature figure of a young girl designed to recline on the bangle's surface." He sketched in the figure. "This will be cast in gold."

Villeneuve nodded and looked at it for several moments. "Your idea is that of the girl floating on the water surface?" Rodin replied "Yes but your question has just given me a new thought. Suppose she were to appear breaking the surface, her torso, head and arms free of the water while her legs were submerged out of sight. The pose would be one of movement as she curved backward as if to re-submerge".

Rodin set up a new sketch and within minutes the idea had been captured most eloquently. "This is better," Rodin said excitedly. "By doing it this way the scale of the figure need not be so small. It even suggests that if she were on the point of re-submerging, the sculpture could be almost a 'bas relief' [semi-two-dimensional]. This would make for a much better interfacing between the gold figure and the silver water." A quick third sketch captured his point. "However, the upraised right arm would be clear of the water and would be fully three-dimensional." A fourth sketch appeared and the upraised arm was shown stretching backward gripping the edge of the bangle giving the sculpture strength.

Villeneuve smiled. "There seems to be a special passion in this creation of yours, Monsieur." Rodin grimaced, "you are right Monsieur Villeneuve … perhaps we should talk business now".

At this moment there was a patter of feet on the stairs at the back and a petite young lady appeared with a swish of skirts making her way swiftly through the shop towards the front door. "Goodbye Papa, I will be back soon." Villeneuve smiled at her proudly and said "Monsieur Rodin may I introduce my eldest daughter, Isabella". Rodin had riveted his eyes on her the moment she appeared (the famous 'Rodin stare'). Isabella smiled and gave a small curtsy and was gone.

"You have a lovely daughter, Monsieur, she moves with such grace – and speed!" They laughed. Villeneuve added "Yes, she is particularly happy just now. She is engaged to an Englishman – Edward Hale – who, I hope, will keep her in this present state of mind. They are soon to be married". Rodin nodded wistfully.

"Lucky man! It must be hard for a father to part with his pride and joy." Villeneuve silently nodded.

After a pause, Rodin now said: "The piece that I have described to you is one of a theme that I call '*Jeune Fille au bain*'. This one is a miniature reclining. Another one in the series is a standing figure that has an overall height of just-under 60 centimeters. There is a third one, that of a seated figure, that I believe I will be selling, in the same scale as the standing one.

"It is the standing figure that was the cause of a great argument between my young assistant and me. To defuse the emotion surrounding this work, I need to take it permanently out of her sight. It is my hope that the bangle I have described to you may convey my message to her that she is forgiven. One day I will tell you the whole story. The point I am making now is that I would like to propose barter – this statue for the finished bangle. Naturally, you will need to see the statue before your commitment is made. I will bring it to London on my next visit."

As Rodin stood up about to depart, Villeneuve said "allow me to introduce my son Frederich". Rodin moved to shake his hand. They shook hands but Frederich remained seated behind his machine and retained a rather sullen expression. Villeneuve gave a small apologetic shrug and escorted Rodin to the door. "It was a pleasure meeting you, Monsieur. I look forward to our next meeting." After Rodin was gone, Villeneuve immediately made a note of his name to make sure he would know it for the next time.

The next opportunity for Rodin to be in London was in March 1885. He had carefully packed the Black Statue in a duffel bag. All spare space in the bag was filled with cushions and pillows for protection. Rodin and the statue arrived in London unscathed. At the first opportunity Rodin made his way to Northampton Square for his second meeting with Villeneuve.

SECOND MEETING – MARCH 17, ~~2006~~ 1885 – 1 p.m.
A blustery day but mostly sunny.

Villeneuve seemed pleased to see Rodin walk through the doorway with his bulky package. Wasting little time on small-talk they proceeded to unwrap the Black Statue. They stood it on the counter. At this time of day, the lighting was quite good. Shafts of sunlight through the Venetian blinds caught part of the counter area.

Villeneuve looked at it for several minutes, shifting it so that it caught the sun. Slowly he rotated the statue to watch the light play across its contours. "This is a lovely piece. It is, of course, your own work, yes?" Rodin nodded but remained silent for a while as Villeneuve continued to examine it. He then lifted it a few inches off the counter. "My word! This is light. It cannot be a metal casting. So I am puzzled by the black coating. It appears to be metal."

Finally Rodin spoke. "What you are looking at is an early experiment with a new technology. No doubt you are familiar with electroplating of small jewelry components; silver on brass, that sort of thing." Villeneuve nodded. "Well, now it is possible to plate larger objects. The work of Edison and Siemens that has led to power generation to light up the cities is also available to run large electroplating facilities." Villeneuve replied, "Yes, but if this is a plating on the surface, what is the plating on? It cannot also be metal, it is too lightweight".

"You are very astute, Monsieur. You have 'hit the head on the nail' as they say. What you are looking at is bronze over plaster!"

"But you cannot plate plaster!" Villeneuve exclaimed.

"Normally that would true," Rodin replied, clearly enjoying his 'cat and mouse' game…. "But I am working with a young friend, an electrician and chemist, who developed a technique which is being called 'Galvano Plastique'. He has a special material that he paints over the plaster surface. This material is 'conductive' to form, what he calls 'the cathode'. Believe me, Monsieur, this is all very technical and I do not fully understand it. However, it works. You are looking at *the first* electroplated plaster cast. There are those who seem aggravated by this development. They are already calling it 'poor-man's bronze'. It is strange how people resent new ideas, is it not?"

"You too, Monsieur Rodin, are very astute. You have 'tagged me' correctly. I have a great interest in new technology. I also have an eye for beauty and I see great beauty in your creation. With this skill you will doubtless be famous some day. You mentioned, at our first meeting, the possibility of barter. I can say that I am more than willing to accept this statue in exchange for my work on the jewelry that we have already discussed. Let us shake hands on this."

Rodin clasped Villeneuve's hand firmly. "On my next visit to London, I will bring the plaster proof of the miniature '*Jeune Fille*' from which you will make a gold casting. Perhaps we can work together as we marry the gold to the silver and finalize our project."

Needless to say, the bangle was completed in time for Rodin to present it to Camille on her 21st birthday, December 8. 1885. Even before her birthday she and Rodin had put the big argument behind them to a fair degree, so the spectacular present created a very happy event. Camille disappeared for a few moments and returned wearing a plain black sleeveless dress. She slipped the bangle over her right hand and glided it slowly up her arm until it came to rest at the delicate swell of her bicep muscle. The fit was perfect.

As Camille entertained Rodin with a number of increasingly seductive poses, he chuckled quietly to himself. The bangle was, *by design, symbolically placed* at the exact position where she had cut off the old arm and replaced it with the modified arm, to irrevocably modify the pose of the controversial, standing, *'Jeune Fille au bain"*.

Rodin, half smiling, now lay back, eyes shut; mused to himself *"I wonder how long it will be before she realizes this?"*

fin.

Footnotes

1 Photographs – Donald Combe, January 2006
2 Photographs – Donald Combe, January 2006

Epilogue

I realized, as my story was approaching a logical conclusion, that I was carrying good news and *less-than-good* news.

The good news, of course, was the firm conviction that we had revealed a unique Claudel/Rodin sculpture - an unsigned, original masterpiece.

The *less-than-good* news was that we had a *hot potato* on our hands. Our little black statue was now of considerable, but unknown, value. *Without authentication from the Musée Rodin in Paris, she was also uninsurable!*

All this combined in my mind to make me further realize that it was time to pass the Black Statue down the line to younger Villeneuve descendents. And so it was that, late in 2005, she was carefully... lovingly... crated and sent on a long journey far from Canadian shores.

Should this book become widely read, it is

perhaps wise that the whereabouts of the Black Statue remain as enigmatic as the statue herself, at least until *a future custodian,* in his or her wisdom, decides otherwise.

Neville Hale. Tuesday, April 25, 2006